The Billionaire's Invitation

Alix Vaughn

Copyright © 2023 by Alix Vaughn

All rights reserved.

No portion of this book may be reproduced in any form without written permission from the publisher or author, except as permitted by U.S. copyright law.

Contents

1. Chapter 1 — 1
2. Chapter 2 — 10
3. Chapter 3 — 18
4. Chapter 4 — 25
5. Chapter 5 — 33
6. Chapter 6 — 40
7. Chapter 7 — 47
8. Chapter 8 — 55
9. Chapter 9 — 63
10. Chapter 10 — 71
11. Chapter 11 — 84
12. Chapter 12 — 92
13. Chapter 13 — 100
14. Chapter 14 — 107
15. Chapter 15 — 115
16. Chapter 16 — 121
17. Chapter 17 — 126

18. Chapter 18	133
19. Chapter 19	141
20. Chapter 20	147
21. Chapter 21	152
22. Chapter 22	161
About Alix Vaughn	172

Chapter 1

Flynn

It's just another ordinary day at the office. On a metal table in the middle of the room lays a synthetic cadaver. It's state-of-the-art, complete with skin, organs, and temperature control. My office has been turned into an operating room.

Over the body stands a tester, wearing VR goggles that make her look like a giant housefly. She is holding suture scissors designed by my head engineer and best friend, Colin Banks. On a tray next to the tester is a collection of different tools designed to be used on the fake body.

This test has not been going well at all. My company, Wired Reality, has been developing an augmented reality system that will replace the need for cadavers in med schools which requires *significant* cooperation from our technology. Not to mention money.

"Can we try the suture again?" Colin asks. "What do you think?" he looks at me, his hazel eyes crimped with worry.

I gesture to the middle of the room. "Floor is yours today."

He grimaces and holds his clipboard tight to his chest as he watches the screen at the far end of the room. "Go ahead, Rickie."

Rickie, his assistant, and the tester today, reaches for another tool on the table. On the screen, I watch her virtual gloved hand hover over the tools. It starts to glitch. Again.

"Fuck," Colin spits and makes a note on his clipboard.

"Want me to keep going?" Rickie asks.

"I guess," he sighs.

"Colin, it's fine," I reassure him, leaning on the edge of my desk. It's *not* fine when we have investors coming in six weeks to look at how far we've come with our progress. But as the CEO of this place, I know that sometimes my team needs encouragement, not a constant kick in the ass.

Colin gives me a look that tells me he doesn't believe me. That's what happens when you work with your friends. It's almost impossible to hide things from each other. Colin and I founded Wired Reality together right out of college, and it has been our brainchild for ten years now. We burst onto the market with reckless abandon, flying high on the ignorance of being amateurs in the cutthroat business world. We tripped our way up the corporate ladder to become a Fortune 500 company.

Now, we have to act like it.

Rickie starts to suture the cadaver. Colin and I watch the screen. "Looks amazing," I say. "How does it feel?"

"The coolant is definitely working," Rickie says, feeling the edges of the open "skin".

Colin smiles and nods, "That's good, that's –"

Suddenly, the screen glitches again, and the suture animation begins scrawling across the screen like an angry black worm.

He throws his clipboard down and runs his hands through his hair. "Fuck it! We're done!"

Rickie pulls her goggles off, her eyes ringed with red imprints like a raccoon.

"Great job, Rick," I say with a sad smile.

She sighs and rubs her forehead. "Thanks."

Colin isn't very good about his temper when things aren't working in his favor. But he's gotten better. I can hear him counting down from ten under his breath in an effort to bring himself back down to earth. "Three... two... one..." He blinks his eyes open, scanning the scene. "Goddammit, Flynn. We're screwed."

"You know why I like you, Colin?" I say, crossing my arms over my chest. "You're so fucking optimistic."

Colin's face sours, but before he can reply, there is a knock at the door. I'm saved from whatever cloud of negativity he's about to spew my way. "Come in!"

My assistant, Wendy, an older woman who still wears her hair in a perm of curls and has signature hot pink lipstick, enters breathlessly. "Mr. Madden, there's a guest here to see you."

I raise an eyebrow. "I wasn't expecting any guests today."

"Normally, I wouldn't interrupt your, um, very important work, but –" She glances towards the table in bewilderment.

Despite wanting to escape Colin's feral anger, I know that leaving right now would just make it worse. "I'm afraid I don't have time for an impromptu guest, Wendy. Feel free to offer them something on my schedule but –"

"Mr. Madden, I really think you're going to want to speak with her."

My ears perk up. Usually, when I have an unannounced guest, it's a man. They feel much more entitled to my time. That's why I prefer to have female investors. "Do I know this visitor?"

Suddenly, I notice Wendy's expression. Deathly. Almost like she's seen a ghost. She nods solemnly.

I frown. No. It couldn't be. "Is it..."

She nods again, more vigorously this time. And that's how I know who is on the other side of that door.

"Flynn."

My eyes shoot to Colin. He knows, too. It's clear by the look on his face.

"You don't have to talk to her."

Oh, but I do. It's been two years since I've been in the same room with her. I tried for months to get her to speak with me, only to be brushed off continuously. Now she's walked right into my office. No doubt wanting to talk. But, about what? I swallow so hard it's audible. "Clear the room, please."

Colin is already a step ahead of me. He knows me too well at this point to think I'm *not* going to talk to the one woman who has been on my mind for two years. He collects his equipment and hustles Rickie out the door with one last look at me over his shoulder. "If you need anything, call. I'll be headed out early to meet Stella, so –"

"I'll be fine."

Colin nods. "You got this."

I try to smile but don't know what I "got". I don't even know what she could possibly want to say to me. Or... what she might want from me.

"Send her in, Wendy," I say softly.

"Right away, sir."

Wendy disappears out the door. I have only a minute to decide where I will receive my guest. Should I sit at the desk, or is that too formal? At the edge of the desk, or is that too posed? At the windowsill, or is that... lame?

By the time I hear the door unlatch again, I haven't moved an inch from the center of the room.

That is where I receive Adelaide Frazer. My ex-girlfriend.

And man, she looks fucking amazing.

Her blonde hair is pulled back into the most perfect, messy bun, strands of hair framing her face as if she's some sort of fairy princess. Her green eyes pop against her slinky, sleeveless olive-colored dress, well-suited for July in NYC.

Every bit of loathing I've had for her since she left me disappears. I can't deny how much I still want her in every way possible.

"Aren't you going to say hello?" she asks, a smirk on her tawny-colored lips.

"Well, of course, I'm going to say..." *Breathe, Flynn.* "Hello, Adelaide. You look well."

Her smirk turns into a grin. Adelaide closes the space between us and grabs my hand. My heart pounds. Fuck, I always hoped when I would see her, I wouldn't care, and yet here I am, ready to fawn all over her. She kisses my cheek gingerly and then retreats. "So do you, Flynn."

"Oh, I'm alright," I say, absent-mindedly rubbing my chin, wishing I had shaved this morning instead of last night.

"Always so self-deprecating," Adelaide says, rolling her eyes.

"It's not hard when you're..." I gesture to her, at a loss for words. Wherever Adelaide goes, she leads with her beauty. And she knows it.

When I met Adelaide Frazer, she was an up-and-coming model. Since then, she's taken catwalks and magazine covers by storm, competing with the likes of the Hadids and Kendall Jenner. I always felt like Roger Rabbit next to her with my glasses and lanky awkwardness.

It turned out I had reason to be worried when our relationship came to a screeching halt after she left me for football player Theo Wadeltsky. Taller, stronger, and objectively more handsome than me.

I just wish she'd had the decency to break up with me before falling into his bed.

Adelaide quirks her head to the side. "Can we sit?"

Stop acting like an idiot. "Yes, of course. Wherever you want."

"I like the new place."

"Thanks. Yeah. We've expanded quite a bit, so we needed to spread out," I say. I guess I have something to show for our two years apart. Wired Reality has grown from an industry name to a household name. Our valuation has skyrocketed, and there's nowhere to go but up.

Adelaide takes a seat in a gray, boxy lounge chair so gracefully it's like she's choreographed the routine.

"Can I get you anything? Water? Coffee?"

"I'll only be a few minutes," she says, waving her hand. "Come sit, come sit."

Of course, she only has a few minutes. When it came to being Adelaide's boyfriend, my life ran on her schedule. Which, as you can imagine, was superbly inconvenient as a CEO of a hugely successful, yet young tech company.

I pour two glasses of water anyway. I'm a busy man too. She doesn't just get to take control of my time like that. "To what do I owe the pleasure of your visit?"

Adelaide reaches into her Chanel purse and produces a cream-colored envelope. "You're officially invited, love."

I ignore the shiver the word "love" sends down my spine and take the envelope, confused. My name is on the back in gold calligraphy.

Oh no.

"What's this?"

"Why don't you open it up and find out."

I split the envelope open and pull out a hefty invitation that sputters golden glitter onto my lap.

You're cordially invited to celebrate the engagement of Adelaide Frazer to Theo Wadeltsky.

"You're engaged," I say, trying to process it.

"I am," she answers excitedly.

I force a smile. "Congratulations."

"We haven't gone public yet, so I hope you'll keep it discreet," Adelaide says, gushing. "Keep reading."

Join Addy and Tee –

I stifle a gag.

On a Mediterranean Cruise, August 1st – 14th.

"A cruise?!" I can't hold back my utter shock. "You want me to come on a cruise with you?"

Adelaide seems nonplussed by my reaction, pulling out a pack of cigarettes from her purse and lighting one up. "Of course. That's why I've invited you, silly."

I try to ignore the swelling smoke wafting into my nose. I never liked the habit, but she says it keeps her skinny. "W-why?"

She sighs and looks off wistfully. "I know things didn't go the best between us, Flynn, but you have to know I care for you. Don't you?"

"Is that why I haven't heard from you in two years?"

Adelaide purses her lips. "We needed time apart."

She needed time away from me to get rid of the guilt. That's how I've always seen it.

"But you were so important to me, Flynn. I grew so much because of you. I've never forgotten that."

"I don't know if that merits an invitation to an engagement party."

She takes a deep inhale of the cigarette. I pray that the sprinklers don't go off. "Of course, it does. I still have love in my heart for you, Flynn. I thought you might feel the same, but..." Adelaide trails off and puts on a face of disappointment. Even though I can see through her antics, I can hardly bear her sadness.

And yet, the hopeless romantic in me wants to say yes without hesitation because two weeks with Adelaide is better than none. Even if she's engaged to another man. But there's another part of me that I can't seem to silence.

What is she getting out of this?

"I still care for you. Of course, I do," I say. I won't be her pathetic ex at her engagement party, though. No way, no how. "I'm just not sure if my girlfriend would approve."

Her eyebrows shoot up, and her green eyes harden like jade. She was just as surprised as me when I said it. "G-girlfriend?"

There is no girlfriend. I'm just doing whatever I can to look like a little bit more of a man in her eyes. "Yes, it's..." I begin and then shrug sheepishly. "We're not public yet, so... discretion. As you said."

Adelaide's laser eyes soften. "Of course."

"You can understand, she probably wouldn't be comfortable with me celebrating your –"

"You'll bring her then, obviously," Adelaide says.

My mouth falls open. "What?"

"You don't need to spare my feelings, Flynn. I'm engaged to another man, for goodness' sake," she says with a laugh, dropping the stub of her cigarette into her untouched glass of water. "Bring her. I'd love to meet her. See if she's good enough for you."

I don't know what to say, so I just stare at her.

"I'm not taking no for an answer. My people will call your people," Adelaide says, rising to her feet. "I've got to run to a fitting in Soho right now."

I stand up quickly. "I'll walk you out."

"No, no, honey. You need to call your girlfriend and tell her you're taking her on the trip of a lifetime."

I don't know if any imaginary or otherwise girlfriend would want to celebrate my ex's engagement with me.

"But before I go, what's her name?" she asks.

"Her name?"

Adelaide scoffs, "Don't act so secretive. I don't need her whole name, Flynn. Just the first one will do."

And I say the first name that comes to mind: "Stella."

"Stella and Flynn. Aww." Adelaide pats my chest. "I'm looking forward to meeting Stella."

I can barely utter a goodbye as she walks out. *What have I just done?*

How am I going to tell my best friend I've just said his little sister is my girlfriend?

Chapter 2

Stella

I look down into the box on the floor, halfway hoping it's empty. But no. As usual, an empty box around here only means one thing.

Puppies or kittens.

Today, it's puppies. Just my luck.

"Hey, little guys. Look at you, huh?" I reach in and wait for one to sniff my hand. A little white pup with a gray splotch over its eye is the lucky winner. I pick him up and cuddle him to my chest. "Goodness gracious, why are you so darn cute?"

The issue with puppies is that they're way more work than kittens. And the work is way more heartbreaking. They're so much more emotional, expressive, and needy.

Sounds familiar.

The shelter is at capacity. In fact, it's over capacity. I took in a senior border collie that was surrendered this morning. Freckles' mom is being moved into memory care and no one can take in the poor pup. How am I going to say no to that?

And now this. Puppies. Lucky for me, puppies go fast, but still. Five more teeny mouths to feed and not enough hands to hold the bottles.

The puppy in my hands is straining to kiss my chin. I giggle and bring him higher so he can reach my face. "Dammit, what do I do with you?"

Animals have always taken a liking to me, and me to them. They're much less complicated than people, even though we don't speak the same languages. That's why I have two dogs at home: Herbie and Otis. And as much as I'd like to take this little guy home, too, I just can't add another animal to my current menagerie.

"We don't have room, Stella."

I look up at Maurice. Maurice is retired but volunteers at the shelter every day. We've become good friends over the last couple of years I've been managing the shelter. He keeps me grounded. "But look at him," I say, holding the little puppy up to Maurice. "Don't you think Rita would love this little guy?"

"You're not pawning another dog off on me, I swear to god, Stella…" he replies, crossing his arms over his chest. However, not even he is immune to puppy kisses, and soon enough, the puppy has wriggled right into Maurice's embrace and he's laughing like he's a little kid. "Seriously, Stella, I can't take another dog. We already have three!"

"Could you just take them home for the night? And then I can think of a plan for tomorrow?" I ask, slowly sliding the box of squeaking pups toward him.

Maurice peers into the box. "Fine," he says with a gruff sigh and then looks at the gray-spotted puppy, "You're lucky you're cute."

One more fire I can put off until tomorrow. That's all this job has been since I started. I never have enough. Funding, volunteers, *space*. When I have to turn animals away, I'm devastated. I've tried to get a thicker skin, but how can you when you're potentially dooming an innocent creature to a kill shelter?

For tonight, though, the puppies and Freckles are safe. As soon as Maurice finishes up his closing duties, I'm left alone with the animals. Just past six in the evening. At the shelter, it's never quiet. Always someone scurrying or sighing. Just the way I like it. I do my rounds, saying bye to the animals. My pups, both former shelter dogs themselves, are waiting for me. It's time to close up shop for today and head home to a nice plate of leftovers and crap TV. Maybe a bath if I –

I hear the beep of the front door opening. Shit. I didn't lock up yet.

I rush out into the front office, shouting, "Sorry, we're closed!" but stop short when I see it's my brother. "Colin, what are you doing here?"

Colin frowns and jerks his thumb out toward his car. "We're having dinner tonight?"

I blink and shake my head like it's an Etch-A-Sketch in an effort to jog my memory. "Oh god. Yeah. That's tonight, isn't it?"

"You forgot again?" Colin asks with a knowing smile.

"I..." I trail off.

He sighs, "Stella, seriously, we need to get you a calendar."

"I have a calendar; I just never use it!"

"Okay, we need to teach you to use a calendar," my older brother teases.

I feel like a complete asshole for forgetting. I'm standing here in ripped jeans, covered in pet hair and slobber, and my brother is still in the suit he wore to the office today. "I can't believe you wear full suits in this heat," I say with a shake of my head.

"Well, next time, you can come to the Village and meet *me* for dinner. I'll wear shorts and a T-shirt, and you won't even recognize me."

I laugh.

"So did I drive out here for nothing, or..."

"No, of course not." No way I made my brother take the ferry to New Jersey just to be sent packing. "Give me a minute and I'll meet you at the car."

"Okay, starting the timer now," he says as he backs out the front door.

I roll my eyes, but I can't ignore a challenge like that. I rush around, finishing my closing routine, the final goodbyes to the animals, and then sprint to his Tesla in the parking lot. I throw myself inside and say breathlessly, "How'd I do?"

"Minute twelve."

"No way."

"Yes way," he says, holding up his watch that's more expensive than a year of my rent.

"You changed it, I bet."

"You'll never know." Colin gives me a mischievous grin and starts to pull the car out of the parking lot.

I stick my tongue out at him and glance back at the shelter as he turns onto the main road. I start to glance back at the shelter, but Colin grabs my arm. "Stella... relax."

I look back at my brother and smile gently. Sometimes it's hard to believe that he's the one working for a Fortune 500 company since he has to bring me back down to earth so much. I know not every day is sunshine and rainbows for him. But he's always taken the job of being my big brother very seriously. Always protective, always loving, and not afraid to give me shit.

I'm lucky to have him.

We go to dinner at Olive Garden. It's been a tradition since we were kids. Every accomplishment came with a trip to Olive Garden. Nowadays, an accomplishment can be as simple as making it through a Monday. Neither of us cares for the fancy schmancy dinners. He begrudgingly goes to plenty of those for work. Olive Garden is just fine for both of us.

Colin always picks up the bill. I know he'd like to pick up quite a bit more. For years now, he's wanted me to capitalize on my biology degree by going to veterinary school, but it's just never been the right time for me to leave the shelter. Of course, when is the right time for anything that takes that much effort?

"The shelter isn't your life, Stella," Colin always reminds me.

However, it has become my life. I think about these animals all the time. And I love them. The pay is shit, of course. I just can't justify leaving them. Or maybe I'm too scared too. If I left, I'd have to think about all the parts of my life that have been left untended. My love life, my friendships, my goals and ambitions (what even are those anymore?)

After dinner, we go to a local ice cream shop and sit out on a plastic picnic table, lapping up ice cream before it melts in the blazing summer heat.

"You think we look strange together?" I ask, glancing at my brother.

Colin frowns. "No, why?"

I give him another up and down. He's removed his suit jacket, thank God, but he's still in his expensive slacks and dress shirt. "I don't know, you don't usually see capitalists and hippies hanging out like this."

Colin laughs heartily. "Well, at the very least, people can tell we're related. It's the hair," he says, pulling on a curly lock of my long hair.

"Hey!" I reach out and grab a curl on his head and yank harder.

"Woah! Easy! You don't know your own strength..." he replies, rubbing the back of his head.

"Serves you right," I say, licking my strawberry ice cream.

Colin shakes his head. "You're a brat."

"Yep. And...?"

He chuckles and we both sit, finishing our ice cream, as the sky swims with orange and pink, the sun getting lower and lower.

"Thanks for coming to visit me," I say eventually.

"Don't I always?"

"Yeah, but I should come up to you, probably."

Colin shrugs. "I prefer you to stay out of the city."

I laugh, "Yeah, I'm much safer in Jersey."

"Better than New York."

"Whatever, bro."

I can feel Colin's eyes harden on me. He gets this look when he's about to say something very parental.

I glare at him. "*What?*"

"What?"

"You're staring at me."

Colin sighs. "I didn't mean to."

"Yes, you did. Say it."

"Say what?"

"What you want to say!" I exclaim and then stuff the bottom of the cone in my mouth, enjoying the melted ice cream mingling with the sweet, crunchy cone.

He folds his hands between his knees and slides them back and forth nervously. "I just wish you weren't so committed to doing everything on your own. "

"What the heck are you talking about?"

"Like going back to school or maybe moving in with me or –"

"You just said you didn't want me in the city," I say pointedly.

Colin groans. "Well, if you *lived* in the city, it would be different."

"*Why* is that different?"

"It just is! You wouldn't be a Jerseyan waltzing in gawking at the skyscrapers."

"I do not gawk."

"Stella, trust me. You're a gawker."

"You don't want me in town. I'd cramp your style."

He snorts. "What style?"

Colin Banks, tech engineer at the biggest company since Tesla. Also, a full-on idiot. "You know. Your big tech bachelor style."

"Eww, okay, I'm taking you home."

I laugh and tease him the whole drive to my apartment. When he parks the car, he gives me a look. "Will you be okay until I see you next?"

"Colin, I'm a grown-ass woman."

"Yeah, and someone has to worry about you. Might as well be me."

I eye my brother. Ever since our parents passed away a few years earlier in a car accident, he's been overprotective. I also feel protective of him, but it's innate in his blood as a big brother to always be making sure I'm alright. "Text me when you get home." I lean over and hug him.

Colin pats my back. "Turn on the light to let me know you're safe."

"You're a worry wart."

"You're correct."

I get out of the car and give him a wave just before I unlock the entryway door. My apartment is up the stairs, the first one on the right. I can already hear the dogs at the door. Herbie, the white pit bull, and Otis, a blonde chihuahua with an underbite, greet me with kisses and impatience to be let out. Before I do anything, I let them out through the kitchen door into the backyard. Then, I hurry to the front window and turn on the table lamp. I wave down at the Tesla even though he can't see me.

As soon as Colin pulls off down the street, I'm left with a sinking feeling.

I do like animals more than people. They give unconditional love and are mostly uncomplicated. I prefer that to humans disappointing me. Specifically, men. After all, what good are they?

And yet, unless it's a rare night I don't have plans, I come home to two beautiful creatures who will never understand me and all my complications.

I haven't let anyone see the real me in a long time. I honestly don't even know how to anymore.

Chapter 3

Flynn

"What do you mean you said you have a girlfriend named *Stella*?"

"Shhh! Lower your voice!" I whisper across the table, scanning the cafeteria to make sure no one is listening in. We met first thing in the morning so I could give him a play-by-play about what happened with Adelaide, and now it's not going so well.

Colin leans his elbow on the table and starts biting on his thumbnail.

"I'm sorry. It just came out," I say, swallowing. "First name I thought of."

"How? How the hell was Stella the first name you thought of?"

I shrug, at a loss. "You had just been in the room, you know. Maybe it was that."

"Rickie was in the room. *Wendy* was in the room. Stella was *not* –"

"I'm just trying to tell you the story, man. It doesn't mean anything, okay?" I try to explain. To be honest, bringing up Stella sort of eludes my comprehension as well. "I just needed a name and I said Stella. It doesn't mean that I'm actually –"

Colin winces before I say anything.

"Dude, seriously."

"You've never hooked up with her, have you? You'd tell me if you did, right?" Colin says, although I'm not sure he'd be able to handle it if the answer were yes.

"Colin, the idea of Stella and me together is *laughable*," I say. Stella is, for all intents and purposes, an anarchist. She's the barefoot, commune-living type. I've spent enough time with her over the years since Colin and I became friends to know that our mutual disdain will always be loud and proud. "Really think about it."

"So, you're saying my sister isn't good enough for you?"

I slap my hands to my face. "Jesus Christ, man!"

Colin pushes some hashbrowns around his plate. "She's not good enough for you."

I gape. "Colin, that's totally not what I said."

"You'd be lucky to have a woman like my sister."

"Do you *want* your sister to be my girlfriend?"

Colin twists his lips to the side and grunts. "Stop."

"Exactly." I can't believe I'm baiting him right back into being annoyed with me. "All I meant was... Stella and I don't get along. You know she hates me."

"She doesn't hate you," Colin retorts.

Time for me to glare.

"I'm just saying. You two have –"

"Irreconcilable differences," I say.

"See, now I'm getting the feeling you're into her again, and now –"

I try to tune Colin out, letting him ramble on about the various thoughts he's having about me and his sister dating when it never has and will never be a thought that crosses my mind. Except for yesterday when I told Adelaide.

I knew from the moment I met Stella that we were... *different*. Now, don't get me wrong, I know opposites do attract. But while Colin and I walked the hallowed halls of Harvard Business School, Stella was doing some peace corps save the world bullshit. I can respect it, but it's not for me.

Unfortunately, the converse is not true. Stella has made it very clear over the years that Wired Reality is just another corporate blemish on the world. The only reason she tolerates Colin's participation is because of their blood relation. So, I'm the lucky recipient of all her political tirades.

Needless to say, we try not to cross paths too often.

"Colin, I can say with absolute sincerity, any man would be lucky to date Stella and we both know as well as anyone that man is *not* me."

Colin narrows his eyes. "And yet you said her name."

I throw my hands up.

"You made this bed, Flynn. "Now you've got to sleep in it," my friend says with a mouthful of hashbrowns.

"Okay, here's the deal. I told Adelaide I have a girlfriend named Stella, and she's expecting me to come on her engagement trip and bring her."

Colin raises an eyebrow. "So?'

"So… I need your help in figuring out what to do, dingus."

"Don't call me a dingus, dingus."

I shut my eyes tight. Thirty-four and I still haven't outgrown the word dingus.

"Just say you can't go."

"I can't do that."

"Why not? You're telling me you're going to go on an unplanned vacation in less than a month?" Colin asks, eyes bugging out.

I understand his shock. We're behind on our deliverables and, while the employees at Wired Reality have unlimited vacation time, Colin and I rarely take advantage of that. There's just always too much going on. "She wants me there."

Colin raises an eyebrow. "Dude. Come on."

"What?"

"Don't tell me this is because you're still carrying a torch for her."

"I'm not 'carrying a torch'."

Colin's expression softens. "You're not totally over it, man. Be honest."

I lean back in my chair and cross my arms over my chest. I feel like my heart has been exposed to the whole cafeteria. "It's been two years. I'm over it."

My friend sighs. "So why do you need to go to her engagement party?"

"To show her I'm over it."

"See, that's how I know you're not over it. If you're still concerned about what she's thinking of you, you're not indifferent to her. You're still hung up."

He has a point. And I know he's right. As much as I wish he wasn't.

"If you go on this trip," Colin starts to say in a tone he saves for explaining new tech to me, "you're opening yourself up to just being consistently hurt having to see how Adelaide has moved on."

"I already have to see that," I mutter. "They're always in the press."

"Then what's the point in going to her *engagement* party if you know it's just going to hurt?"

Maybe I'm a masochist of the heart. By going on this trip, I'm just opening myself up to be hurt even more than I already have been by her betrayal. While I know I'd be indulging the part of myself that doesn't want to let go of the ache, I can't shake the gut feeling that I have to go.

"You're going to go no matter what, aren't you?"

I half-laugh. "You know me too well."

Colin leans forward and ruffles his hands through his curly brown hair, cursing under his breath. "Okay. Fine. How can I help?"

I smile nervously. "Well, I need a Stella."

"Don't even think about –"

"You won't even let me ask?"

"That's my sister!"

"You've made that very clear!"

Colin huffs, stuttering as he tries to find something to say. "You could hire someone. An actress. This is New York, for God's sake."

"You know that it would fall through," I say. "It would take literally one Google search to find the girl's headshot and resume."

Colin rubs his temples. "Can't you just lie and say you said a different name?"

"Gaslight her?!"

"Oh, come on, it's not like she wouldn't deserve it. She isn't exactly a saint, Flynn."

Colin does have a point there. "I like to take the high road."

"You're not taking Stella."

I wring my hands and anxiously crack my knuckles. "You know nothing would happen."

"Uh-uh-uh. You say that now. But you two would have to pretend to be a couple and that would involve some stomach-churning hand-holding and cheek kisses and –" Colin presses his hand to his mouth. "I'm getting sick just thinking about it."

I know this is a stretch. I got myself into this mess and I should work on getting myself out of it instead of committing to the godforsaken bit. But at this point, the only way out is through. "Couldn't she use a vacation? It's two weeks in the Med."

Colin stops; I see the cogs turning in his head. He's... considering. *Yes.* "You'd pay for everything."

I withhold a smile. I feel like he's on the verge of agreeing. "Of course. Without a doubt."

"And you wouldn't –"

I wave my hands through the air. "Wouldn't dream of it. She looks too much like my best friend anyway."

Colin kicks me under the table. I may have deserved that. But it's the truth. They have the same curly brown hair and matching hazel eyes, although Stella's are more flecked with amber while Colin's lean more toward green. "So...what do you think?" I ask as I rub my shin.

He looks out the window at the tiny streets below. Maybe wishing he were anywhere in New York but here. "Fine. You can ask her."

"Would you go with me to, you know, mediate?"

Colin scoffs. "I'll go with you to Jersey, but I'll be damned if I participate in that conversation."

I nod. That's more than I deserve. "I owe you."

Colin narrows his eyes at me. "But if she says no, you can't beg."

I can't make a promise that I won't beg at least a little, but I nod. "Deal."

"And if she agrees, you better make sure she doesn't get into any trouble. I know how those people can be."

"Any trouble she gets into will be of her own accord."

"*Flynn.*"

"What?! Stella's a free spirit. Isn't that in her Instagram bio? Stella's gonna do what Stella is gonna do."

Colin hums. He knows I have a point there. "And you'll be a perfect gentleman the whole time."

"When haven't I been?"

Colin lowers his chin, eyes nearly rolling back all the way into his head. "I'd like to inform you that every time you think you've gotten away with a quickie at the office, you haven't."

I open my mouth to respond, but I have nothing to say.

"I need you to be a gentleman for real this time, Flynn." Colin holds his hand out across the table. "Shake on it."

I grab his hand and shake firmly. "You have no reason to worry, Colin."

He pulls his napkin off his lap, bunches it up, and throws it down on the table before getting up. "Oh, I know I don't. There's a ninety percent chance that Stella tells you to 'fuck off' before you even get your question out," he says with a laugh. "Meet me in the garage at four pm sharp."

"Today?"

"Yes, Flynn. You're going to ask my sister to be your fake girlfriend today," Colin says, nearly gagging on the words. Then, he walks off without another word, leaving me to clean up our trays.

Now, how the hell am I going to get Stella Banks to come on a two-week vacation with me as my fake girlfriend when I know she hates my guts?

I've got until four to figure it out.

Chapter 4

Stella

I am happily helping the three new puppies, currently named Snap, Crackle, and Pop, nurse on baby bottles jerry-rigged into a milk crate. It's positioned on a slant so they can sit their little butts down and let gravity do the work of getting the milk into their little bellies.

The gray one that went home with Maurice is *staying* home with Maurice, thank goodness. Rita took such a shine to the little guy, as did the three other rescues they already have at home. One puppy down, three to go. Hoping to have these little guys in homes by the end of the week.

Then, there's sweet Freckles. She's graying around the snout and seems to keep mostly to herself, still mourning the loss of her owner. It breaks my heart to see her. The only time she's eager for pets is when I have handfuls of treats. I'm already foreseeing a future where she's stuck here six months down the line. We give them all the love we can, but every animal deserves to live their last days in a happy home, not here at the shelter.

It's the thick of the afternoon, but there's a nice breeze in the air which makes sitting outside with the dogs extremely pleasant. Some of them are roaming around, others have found a patch of sun in which to take a nap, and others are playing with some of the volunteers.

Snap gets confused and starts pushing his sister Crackle off of her bottle. I have to pick up his wiggly body and readjust. "There you go, Snap. Let your sister eat in peace."

Typical boy.

"Jeez, that's a lot of dogs."

My body goes rigid at the sound of his voice. God *that voice*. Flynn Madden. The embodiment of devil's advocate, aka the worst kind of person. The only reason I've ever put up with him is because he's been my brother's best friend since their very first day of college.

What the hell is that voice doing here?

I whip around and see Flynn and Colin standing on the patio overlooking the yard where all the animals are frolicking. Some dogs have already noticed them and are tromping up for pets and scratches. Colin is happy to give them. Flynn, on the other hand, is flustered. Someone must have let them through because they recognized Colin.

"Can I help you?" I call out with a bewildered expression.

"There she is," Colin says. His expression looks rather grim. I can't imagine what kind of news he's delivering or what he might need from me with an expression like that. He forces a smile as he leads Flynn over to me. "Hey, sis."

I'm about to reply, but we're interrupted when Flynn groans. He picks up his foot, dog shit plastered to the bottom of his leather shoe. I laugh loudly. "Gotta be careful where you step around here!"

Flynn laughs without smiling and pulls a handkerchief out of his pocket to wipe off the bottom of his shoe. If I didn't think Flynn was an east coast WASP before, the handkerchief really pushed him over the edge.

"To what do I owe the... I'd say pleasure, but I'm not sure that's why you're here," I say, quirking my eyebrows at my brother.

"Can't a guy come to play with some dogs?" Colin tries to smile.

"A guy," I gesture to Colin, "can. But that guy –" I then gesture to Flynn. "He doesn't seem like the playing-with-dogs type."

Colin looks back at Flynn who is now holding out the handkerchief, unsure what to do with it. He sighs heavily. "Just know that this wasn't my idea, okay?"

I reposition Snap and Crackle again. "Why are you being so cryptic?"

"What do I do with this?" Flynn asks, desperation in his blue eyes.

"I'll take it. You talk to her," Colin says. He snatches the handkerchief from Flynn, holding it a foot away, and goes to dispose of it. A few of the dogs follow at his heels and Colin starts to make a game of it.

This leaves me with Flynn. He stares down at the box of puppies. "That's quite a contraption."

"Easier than doing it one at a time."

"I can imagine. How old are they?"

I don't know why he's trying to be pleasant or why he's feigning curiosity about my work, an interest he's never really had before. I've always been a do-gooder in his eyes, sacrificing my education and potential to spend my day petting animals. If only he knew how complicated this job really was. "From the looks of it, about eight weeks. Hard to be sure. Someone found them in a box on the side of the road and brought them in last night."

"Wow."

"Yeah."

This is extremely awkward. I can't help but shake what Colin said: *This wasn't my idea*. What the hell am I in for? "What are you doing here, Flynn? Interested in adopting?"

Flynn laughs. "No. No, animals aren't my thing."

"Hm, would have never guessed," I say sarcastically. Once again, I have to move Snap off of Crackle's bottle. "Seriously, dude…"

To my surprise, Flynn hikes up the fronts of his slacks and plops himself on the ground across from me. "I actually came to talk to you."

I don't take my eyes off the dogs. "About what?"

"Um…well…" He half-laughs to himself. I remain stoic. "It's a funny story, actually."

"Is it?"

Flynn's blue eyes flick to mine and for a brief second, my heart leaps into my throat. I've never been able to ignore that he's an attractive man. He just lacks a personality to match. Always chasing after model types and making his work his personality. "I… you remember Adelaide, right?"

"How could I forget?" Adelaide Frazer, supermodel ex-girlfriend. Never met the woman, thank God, but spent plenty of time hearing Colin complain about her.

"Well, she's getting married, and she's invited me to her engagement party."

I feel myself soften. Flynn's expression is full of… shame. I might not like him, but as my brother's best friend, I hated to see what Adelaide did to him. "God, she's such a narcissist."

"Well –"

"Like she still wants your attention after all this time. That's so lame."

Flynn chuckles. "It is lame, I guess." He looks down at his shoes, a lock of black hair falling out of place.

"Don't tell me you're going…" I say even though I know the answer. He sighs. "Yeah, I am."

"No, Flynn. You're much better than that."

"Well, apparently not." Flynn half-smiles at me. "To make matters worse, it's a two-week cruise."

I groan. "Oh god, you're kidding."

"Nope."

"You rich people…"

Flynn doesn't get a chance to respond before Freckles nudges her black and white snout up against his shoulder. "Oh, hi," he replies, leaning away.

Freckles tries to lick his chin, but he's just out of reach. So, she crawls into his lap.

I smile. "She likes you."

"Apparently," he replies dodging her eager tongue.

I reach out and scratch her side. "She doesn't like anybody."

"So, you're saying it's a compliment."

"Or she just has bad taste," I say dryly.

Flynn rolls his eyes, attempting to tame Freckles' affection with head scratches. "Ha, ha."

For a moment, we are quiet, focused entirely on Freckles. Perhaps she's the type to like a withholding sort of guy. Flynn walked in and acted like none of the dogs mattered and now here she is licking his chin like they're old friends. And Flynn likes it too. He's actually smiling and looks relaxed. That's the power of a furry friend. "So… you came out here to tell me you're going to your ex's engagement party?" I finally ask.

Flynn's body goes rigid. "That's where the story gets funny."

"*That's* where the story gets funny, okay…"

"I sort of told her I had a girlfriend. And she invited her to come along."

I frown. "You don't have a girlfriend though, right?" At least not one that I know of.

Flynn takes a break from petting Freckles to adjust his glasses. "Right... that's sort of my predicament."

An uneasy feeling swells in my stomach. Especially when I see how his blue eyes are boring into mine. "Why are you looking at me like that?"

"I need someone to pretend to be my girlfriend."

I'm so stunned I don't even notice that Snap, Crackle, and Pop are still sucking on empty bottles of milk until Pop takes a tumble trying to hop up onto my leg. "I – oh my god –" I grab the little guy and hold him to my chest, like he's suddenly an emotional support dog. "You're not about to ask me, are you?"

Flynn glances over his shoulder at Colin who is trapped in a cuddle puddle with a bunch of dogs. "Look, I know it's... unconventional."

"Oh, my God." I squeeze Pop tighter to my chest and he whimpers. "Sorry, little guy." I drop him back down with the other pups while they all flounder together.

"But it's just two weeks."

I stare at Flynn dumbfounded. "No."

"What?"

"I'm not going to pretend to be your girlfriend. Are you insane?" I start to pull the finished bottles out of their holder.

"Stella, please, you have no idea how –"

"Flynn, I'm not doing it. There are plenty of women who would be falling over each other to spend two weeks with you," I say firmly as I get to my feet. "Sorry you came all the way out here for nothing, but..." I trail off and then head back inside to go wash the bottles.

Flynn, however, is not willing to let up. "Stella, you're the only woman I know that I could actually pull this off with. We have a rapport. A history!"

"Not *that* kind of history," I retort.

He follows me into the kitchen. "You know what I mean. We've known each other for years. It'd be believable that we might have some sort of relationship. I can't fake it with just anyone."

I'm so fucking pissed. I can't believe Colin brought Flynn out here just for this. What was he thinking? I drop the bottles in the sink and turn on the water. The sink sputters and then starts dripping with dark brown water. "Un-fucking-believable."

"Think of it as a vacation! You get two weeks in the Mediterranean, all expenses paid, everything on my tab and –"

"I am not about to do an amateur theatrical production while stuck with you on a boat pretending to be your girlfriend, Flynn! That's absolutely –"

"What do you want in return?" Flynn interrupts me loudly.

And that question gives me pause.

"How much do you want? A couple grand? Or –" He sighs. "Please Stella, I'll do whatever you want if you'll just agree to do this with me."

I chew on my lower lip as I consider Flynn's desperation. Flynn and Colin have been on the cover of every business magazine, back-to-back clad in their suits, staring at you like they know they could buy your tiny little life right out from under you. And right now, he looks like he's about to fall apart.

God, this guy is a mess.

"An anonymous donation. To the shelter," I say. "We need all kinds of repairs. Plumbing. The roof. And I'd like to build an addition so we can house more animals."

Flynn's eyes move back and forth as he figures out what that's going to cost him. "Okay. Deal."

"And..."

"What?" he asks, visibly wincing at what I might do to his checkbook.

"You're taking *her* home," I say, pointing at Freckles who, unbeknownst to us both, followed Flynn inside.

Flynn looks down at the old border collie. Freckles noses at his knee, looking for pets. He returns his gaze to me. "Seriously?"

I cross my arms. "You want me as your fake girlfriend or not?"

He grunts and crouches down to Freckles level. "Looks like you're coming home with me, girl."

Freckles' tail wags back and forth and her tongue lolls out of her mouth. This has gone better than I expected. "So," I say with a smirk. "When do I need my bags packed, babe?"

Flynn's eyebrows jump up, clearly shocked I'm already in character.

This is going to be fun. Or a complete disaster.

Chapter 5

Flynn

I check my watch for the umpteenth time in the ten minutes I've been standing here. Stella's not even late, but I'm terribly anxious. What if she changed her mind and went back to the States? What if I'm going to be left standing here on a dock at the Port of Piraeus, already sweating in the Grecian heat, doomed to have to force a smile for two weeks while I watch my ex-girlfriend tromp around with her brain-dead fiancé?

I start tapping my foot anxiously and pull out my phone to check our text messages back and forth.

The last one was sent about an hour ago.

Waiting for car now.

But she never said *if* she got in the car. What if while she was waiting she said fuck it and fuck Flynn, I'm going home. That's not out of the realm of possibility for her.

I knew we should have flown out together. But I wanted to have a day in Athens to rest before this trip which will doubtlessly be the death of me. Stella couldn't join me, wanting to make sure the shelter was prepared to deal with her absence. She has not let me forget that she's taking vacation time and sick days in order to go on this trip with me.

I have to make it worth her while.

Just breathe, Flynn. Traffic in Greece is horrible. Right? Isn't that a thing?

I scratch my jaw which is smooth, if not a little irritated from shaving first thing this morning. I stare out at the blue-green waters. I've never been one for yachting, but that's a requirement when it comes to the lifestyle I've chosen. Two weeks on a boat is... not ideal. I'm already picturing myself knocking my head on a low doorframe or the showerhead.

Even the most mega of yachts fail to cater to us tall guys.

The boat is docked a little down the way. I've managed to stay out of sight, not wanting to be recognized by any of Adelaide's old friends. I've been watching as a steward with space buns is greeting guests at the gangplank while the crew is grabbing the overabundance of luggage.

I have had a few weeks to prepare for this. But there's not enough preparation in the world that could make this situation any easier.

"Flynn!"

I leap into the air at the shock of hearing my name. "Christ!" I turn around and find Stella rushing down the dock toward me. Her brown curls are pulled back into a messy mop on her head and sweat is dripping off her brow. More noticeable, though, is her outfit. Striped overalls that make her look like a fucking train conductor over a light cotton blouse that is so see-through I can make out the shadow of her collarbone through it. And some beat-up Tevas. Dear God.

"I was – looking for you –" she says breathlessly, skittering to a stop in front of me with her bright purple suitcase. "Didn't you – my calls –"

"Your calls?"

"I was calling, I couldn't – couldn't find – "

I pull my phone out and notice I don't have any bars. "Shit, I didn't have service. I'm sorry, I –"

"No worries. It's..." Stella holds up her hand. *Give me a minute.* She grabs her shirt and fans it away from her chest. "Jesus Christ it's hot here."

"It's the Med."

"*It's the Med,*" she replies in a mocking tone.

I roll my eyes. This is already off to a bad start. "You know you can't talk to me like that once we're on the boat. We talked about this."

"I know, I know. I'm just getting it out of my system," she says, then takes a deep breath, putting on a serene smile. "Okay, I'm better now. Hello, honey."

My body braces at her term of endearment. She always says it facetiously, but it does feel nice to have someone call me that, even if we're faking. "Hello, dear."

"Dear? How old are we, Flynn?"

"What do you want me to call you? Darling? Lover?"

"Lover?! Eww! That's so –"

"*Stella,*" I scold, taking a step closer to her. "What did I say?"

She demurs her head to the side, fluttering her lashes. "Even people in a relationship give each other shit, Flynn."

I suddenly realize how close I've gotten to her. I can smell her perfume mixed with her sweat, sweet and salty at once. It's... intoxicating. I clear my throat and take a step back. "Just don't make a sour face when I try to be sweet to you, alright?"

"Then don't look like I've just kneed you in the balls when I call you 'honey'," Stella says dryly.

Is that really how I looked when she said it?

Stella nods her head toward the yacht. "That the boat?" Then, she starts walking in that direction.

I follow her, dragging my suitcase behind me. "Woah, slow down."

"Why? Doesn't it leave port in half an hour?"

"Stella, we need to talk about what you're wearing," I say. Even though she's set a quick pace, my long legs keep me on an even keel.

"Oh yeah, it's cute, right?" she says with a sneaking smile.

I try not to let my frustration be visible as we close in on the steward. "What happened to the wardrobe I got you?"

"Relax, it's packed," Stella says. "I just got off an international flight. I wanted to be comfortable."

I glance down at her ridiculous purple suitcase. "You could have changed in the airport. I want you to make a good impression."

Stella snorts in laughter. "Wow, are you telling me I don't look nice?"

"Yes, that's exactly what I'm telling you." It's not fair of me to say, but it's true. In other circumstances, I would say she looks… well, I'd never describe Stella as beautiful for fear of being castrated by her brother, but there is something about her au naturelle look that's always made me look a little too long at her. "Stella, these people are piranhas. If you're not up to date with your fashion, your tech, your politics, they're going to eat you alive."

She smirks. "Flynn, do you trust me?"

I take a pause.

"You trust me enough to be your girlfriend for two weeks," she says in a voice low enough for only me to hear over the wheels of our suitcases. "Right?"

"I guess that's true."

Stella slows down as we approach the boat steward, a bold grin creeping over her lips to greet them. "Then trust me when I say that I can handle myself."

"Wait, wait, wait –" I stop just short of the steward being able to greet us. "This isn't about *you* Stella. This is about me. I'm trying to make a good impression on…" I gesture to the boat and stop speaking. "You know?"

Stella's hazel eyes glint and she cocks her head to the side, a few curls falling askew. "Why are you so hung up on her?"

"I'm not hung up," I whisper.

"Well, you care an awful lot about what she thinks of you," Stella retorts, crossing her arms over her chest and leaning into her hip.

"I care what everyone thinks about me."

"That's not true and you know it."

Her words hit me like a ton of bricks. Stella is not shy about being direct and to the point. She also knows how to cut right to the heart of the matter without really considering if someone is ready to acknowledge the truth.

"She left you, Flynn. She embarrassed you. And you… why do you care about what she thinks? She's a bad person."

I feel an impulse to defend Adelaide, but I hold my tongue. I don't want this conversation to continue any longer. "Come on, we have a boat to catch."

Stella sighs. "Alright. Let's do this."

We are greeted by the crew who have been idling, waiting for us to wade through our bullshit so they can greet us. After the crew takes our bags, the steward directs us up the long gangplank. It feels like I'm entering the underworld. A beautiful, blissful façade.

On the deck, we are greeted by another stew and the captain, an older man with white hair and a matching beard. "Captain Karakas," he says with a light Grecian lilt. "Welcome aboard the Thessalonica."

The stew gives us both glasses of champagne. "Everyone is on the aft deck," she explains with a gesture down the length of the boat.

We thank her and then head down the deck.

"Take my arm," Stella says, slipping her hand into the crook of my elbow.

I don't say anything, chewing on the inside of my lower lip, trying to decide what I'm going to say when I see Adelaide again. I've gone through this moment over and over since I accepted the invitation. And it's never gone right in my head.

"Don't be nervous," Stella murmurs like she can read my mind. "You look great, you've got a cute girl on your arm, and you're literally a billionaire. What's she got? Legs for days? So what?"

I laugh despite my nerves. I guess all of those things are true, although I didn't know that Stella thought I looked great too.

That feels nicer than it should.

"Say something that makes me laugh," Stella says, tugging on my arm.

"What?"

Stella bursts out laughing as we walk out onto the aft deck. "Stop it, you're ridiculous."

I laugh too, trying to keep my eyes on her even though I can feel Adelaide's presence pulling my gaze toward her like a magnet.

"Well, look who it is!" Adelaide announces loudly to the group that is already gathered.

Finally, I look over at her, and… she's stunning. What can I say? All legs and arms, her blonde hair is now done in perfect curls down her shoulders, a macrame dress that shows off pieces of her tanned skin underneath.

Too bad she's standing next to the boulder of muscle that is her fiancé.

"So glad you could come, darling." Adelaide struts over to me and gives me kisses on both of my cheeks. Then she looks down at Stella, lips perked, and eyebrow raised. "Is this Stella?"

"That's me," Stella says. I detect a little edge of nervousness in her voice. Even she can't always be full of swagger. Stella sticks her hand out toward Adelaide. "Nice to meet you."

Adelaide eyes Stella's hand and then takes it limply. The judgment is pouring off of her, palpable like rain falling from a gutter. "Well, she's just charming, isn't she?" she says to me. "I'm looking forward to getting to know you, Stella. This is a special man."

Not my heart fluttering at that.

"He is. I'm lucky you got rid of him," Stella says, leaning into me and patting my chest.

"Jeez, thanks, Stell."

Adelaide forces a laugh and then gestures to the rest of the guests. "Well, now that we're all here, how about a toast?" She returns to her fiancé and the two of them start some sickly-sweet toast about their love and how special it is that they can share this moment with their closest friends. I don't know why I'm included when the guest list is so exclusive.

"Thanks," I whisper in Stella's ear.

She smirks and knocks her hip against mine. "No problem."

"Psst."

We look over at the woman standing nearest us. A stunning woman with bright red lipstick and futuristic sunglasses.

"Your dungarees are amazing," she murmurs to Stella in an Australian accent.

Stella squeezes my arm tight. "Thanks. I got them on sale."

Maybe this is going to go better than I thought.

Chapter 6

Stella

Dinner is an amazing feast. Somehow, they've managed to cram all of us down a long banquet table on the aft deck. I'm wedged in between Flynn and a football player. Or should I say soccer? The groom is an American footballer but for some reason, he has a close friend who is a British footballer. I'm trying not to get too bothered with all the details since all of these people are going to be mere memories in two weeks' time.

We're seated right at the head of the table near the happy couple. At first, I wasn't sure why, but now that I've watched how Flynn fawns over Adelaide, I get it. She's just making him suffer.

"How long have you two been together?" Adelaide asks, brushing a hand through her hair.

I take a deep breath. Flynn and I went through all the details. We both know this answer. "Five months," we answer in unison.

"Oh shit, you've already got the same brain," Theo, her fiancé, whose neck is so thick he looks like a thumb, doltishly laughs.

Flynn and I exchange a look.

"You're Colin's sister, right?" Adelaide asks.

"You remembered," Flynn says as if remembering the name of his best friend's sister merits a Fulbright.

"'Course I did, silly."

Barf.

"I didn't remember you by name, but when I saw the names on the RSVP, I could put two and two together." Adelaide's green eyes zero in on me. "I can't imagine Colin was too happy to see you move in on his best friend."

I start to speak, but Flynn takes over. "It was me, actually. I was the one who made the move and… yeah."

"He had Colin's blessing," I add.

"I mean you've known each other for years, right? What made you want to make a move after all that time?" Adelaide pushes her fork around her plate, eyeing Flynn carefully.

Flynn pauses. Any sort of emotionality or sense of romance we left out any sort of emotionality or sense of romance when we talked through the "relationship planning". After all, this is a business transaction more than anything. "Well, she's a very compassionate person. And you know how hard it can be to find people like that when you're always in the public eye."

Zing.

"She doesn't give a shit about pretense. For better or worse, I guess," Flynn says with a chuckle. "Grounds me."

Those were… nice things to say about me. I don't know if he believes them, but the compliments are appreciated.

"Aw, that's sweet. Isn't that sweet Tee?" Adelaide asks, leaning herself onto her future husband's broad shoulders. "Why did you ask me out?"

I can see Flynn wince out of the corner of my eye.

"Because… I mean, your Instagram. Have you seen yourself?" Theo says, looking to his soccer buddy for support. The two of them laugh.

Adelaide's face sours. "Well, anyway –"

"Yeah, anyway…" Flynn says. I wouldn't blame him if he lost his appetite after that.

"How is Colin, by the way?" Adelaide asks me.

I keep the conversation on Colin for a good, long, boring while. I love my brother, but his work sounds hellish compared to getting to hang out with dogs. Lucky for me, I can filibuster like a politician and watch as Adelaide gets bored to tears, wishing she had sat literally *anyone* else in the two seats beside her.

Dinner goes on, and different conversations spark up around the table like fireworks. I'd love an earful of each one.

I recognize some of the faces. Two women at the end of the table are also models, Brandy Mars and Chiana Baresi. I wouldn't have been able to name them off the top of my head, but when we were introduced, I recognized the names. Brandy brought her girlfriend, Sloan Baylor, a famous pop musician with a spikey blonde cut whose music I hate (I of course told her it was an honor to meet her). Then there are a couple of Theo's teammates and their wives who all have the whitest veneers I've ever seen.

And then there's me and Flynn.

A strange amalgamation of people if you ask me.

"Alright, you're my new star."

I look across the table at the woman who complimented me earlier. Cash Cole. Not to be forgotten. I knew the name, but always thought Cash was a man. It turns out, Cash Cole is a gorgeous, diminutive Aussie who truly gives off goddess vibes. "Beg your pardon?" I ask.

"Your style. It's magnificent. Isn't it, Gregory?"

Gregory, I've come to understand, is her assistant. A stocky man with a dangling earring and hair bleached so blond it's silver. "Magnificent," he replies. His talent is repeating exactly what she says back to her.

Cushy job.

"Well, thank you," I say, giving Flynn a smug smile. We had an argument in our cabin earlier over what I should wear. Tension was rife since we realized we were going to have to share a queen bed rather than the king we both expected. I swear if he even so much as nudges me in the middle of the night, I'm filing a lawsuit. "Did you hear that, Flynn?"

"I did," he says before taking a forkful of cucumber salad.

I glance down at my dress, a green bohemian gown with a lace-up front I got at a Renaissance Faire years ago. I think it makes my tits look amazing. I'd rather wear things that I know will make me feel amazing than all the expensive luxury shit Flynn bought for me. If I'm not confident in it, it's not going to look good. That's just my philosophy.

"It really embodies what we're going for in our next collection, don't you think, Gregory?"

"Yes, really embodies what we're going for."

Cash, from what Flynn told me after we made the rounds of meeting everyone during the champagne toast, used to be the head designer for Buq but then branched out to make her own eponymous brand that has both a luxury and more commercial market.

"Spring trends are going to be very bohemian, very Dungeons and Dragons chic, you know?" Cash explains.

Flynn laughs into his napkin.

She's not far off base with my Ren Faire dress.

"You know, we want medieval without the plague," Cash explains.

"Yes, no plague," Gregory adds.

"I can assure you this is the first time that Stella is ahead of the trends," Flynn remarks.

I step on his toe under the table. "Don't be rude, *dear*," I say with a grin.

"It's a compliment really, *darling*," he says, putting his arm on the back of my chair. "Stella marches to the beat of her own drum."

"That much is obvious," Adelaide pops out from the head of the table.

I withhold a glare.

Unless she's trying to rub salt in the wound.

"Well, I can tell," Cash says to Adelaide. Apparently, Adelaide has spent some time as Cash's favorite model. "There's something so delicious about it. Someone unafraid to show up as her full self. Comfortable shoes and all."

My toes curl in my Tevas. Flynn laughs some more. "Shut up," I say, shoving him on the shoulder harder than is probably "cute".

"Yes, shut up, Flynn. You showed up in the same linen suit every other man here is wearing. Stella *dared*."

"Well, I don't know about that, but –"

"Hush," Cash interrupts. "You're my new icon."

I can feel Adelaide glowering at me from the head of the table.

"Have you ever modeled?"

My eyes widen. "Uh, no."

"She's lying, Flynn?" Cash points at Flynn with her fork.

"Uh…" Flynn glances at me.

"I haven't! Swear to God," I intervene quickly and then sip my small glass of ouzo, grimacing at the flavor of anise.

Cash shakes her head. "That's criminal."

"Criminal," Gregory echoes.

"I agree," Flynn says.

I do a double take. "What?"

"I mean…" He shrugs. He's just being nice because he has to be. Because we must feign attraction and *love*. "I think you'd be a great model."

"No, that's silly," I reply, swiping my fork through the last bit of tabouli on my plate.

Flynn shakes his head adamantly. "No, you're selling yourself short."

I don't know how to reply. I'd like this part of the conversation to be over for fear of growing as red as a radish.

"Don't look so surprised. This is your boyfriend, isn't it?" Cash teases me.

No. "Yes, I know, just –" I glance at Adelaide. Time to appease the evil queen. "Modeling isn't just something everyone can do."

Adelaide smiles smugly. "She's right."

"Well, you don't have to be a supermodel. You could have someone take pictures of you. I think you'd be…" Flynn trails off, his blue eyes in mine. "You'd be good at it."

My heart is thumping in my chest. He's a very good actor. Or maybe…

"Flynn's exactly right. And you also don't have to be a supermodel to walk on a runway. Which is why I'm going to insist that you walk in my show in September."

I nearly spit out my tabouli. "What?!"

"Right, Gregory? I insist."

"She insists," Gregory adds.

I shake my head. "I couldn't possibly."

"Don't be silly. You're doing it. Tell her, Flynn." Cash snaps at Flynn.

I can't even look at him. I'm half-hoping he'll come to my defense by saying that I'm an ugly ogre who doesn't belong on a runway.

Instead, he adjusts his glasses and then says carefully, "I think you'd be great. You should do it."

I look up at him.

"I mean, you're gorgeous," he goes on. It doesn't come out as forced as I would expect. "And I've seen the way you walk over to break up dogs who are playing too roughly."

I laugh loudly. "How does it look?"

"Well, when I see it, I think 'Giselle Bundchen who?'"

I laugh even harder, touching his arm. It's both to uplift our false narrative and because I don't mind being close to him as much as I thought I would.

"You two are adorable, aren't they?" Cash says, leaning back in her chair.

Gregory concurs. "Very."

I look over at Adelaide. She looks like she could laser me off the earth from the intensity of her stare. And it doesn't scare me one bit.

I've realized my purpose here. Moreso than pretending to be Flynn's girlfriend, I'm here to protect him. Whether he knows it or not. So, if he's going to be putty in her hand, I'm going to be the exact opposite. I'm going to be the thorn in her side.

"Okay," I finally say. "Sure, why not?"

Cash and Gregory cheer. Flynn puts his hand on my upper back, sliding it back and forth tenderly. Maybe he really does like me. Or care about me.

I'm shocked that when he draws his hand away, I wish he'd kept it there.

Chapter 7

Flynn

"We've managed to work out most of the bugs, but for some reason, the program is shutting down after fifteen minutes."

I sigh as I pace back and forth on the pool deck. "Well, that's not good."

"Understatement," Colin retorts. "How's the party?"

I glance up at the view. We've started off the engagement tour at Santorini. White buildings with blue roofs pepper the hillside while the blue sea sparkles with the midday sun. "We've made our first stop in Santorini. Pool day," I say dryly.

"You say that like it's a punishment."

I wish I could enjoy it. But my mind has been racing ever since I landed in Athens. There's always something to think about that is taking me from the present moment. For one, leaving Wired Reality behind wasn't the smartest move. We are supposed to be providing our investors with a finished product by September for a projected first-quarter release next fiscal year.

For another, the whole reason I'm here is Adelaide. She's been on my mind persistently since we arrived, even when I'm not near her. Sometimes I feel my blood boil thinking about her and Theo in the master suite together doing God knows what. Other times, I feel my heart break in two at what an utter fool I am to attend my ex-girlfriend's engagement party.

And finally, there's Stella. I was worried I'd have to keep tabs on her and make sure she's not saying something ridiculous that's going to blow our cover. Instead, I'm just flabbergasted at how she's fit right in with some of the guests, specifically Cash, who seems to find Stella completely enchanting.

All those things together have me walking through a haze. I'm standing in one of the most beautiful places on earth and can't even see through my own bullshit.

"You think it might have been a mistake?" Colin asks.

"No," I say firmly and quickly. "No, not at all."

"What's your goal by being there? You're trying to break Theo and Adelaide up?"

"No." Not in so many words, but there is a sliver of hope in me that being around me for two weeks is going to make Adelaide realize what a mistake she's made. "More like… exposure therapy." *Stop lying to yourself, Flynn.*

I feel a splash of water at my ankles and look down into the pool. Stella pokes up her head from the water. She's the only girl at the party that's gotten her hair wet. In fact, she's the only one actually swimming. Adelaide and her friends are laying out tanning, Cash is bouncing around on a lounge floatie, and Stella is flailing around like a mermaid. "Hey! Get off the phone!" she says, wiping water out of her eyes.

"It's your brother," I say with a smile.

Stella folds her arms on the edge of the pool. Her curls are tied back in a big bun, dripping with water. "Tell him I say hi and that you have to get off the phone!"

"Stella, we're talking about business things, I can't just –" I begin.

Colin quickly cuts me off. "Is she telling you to get off the phone? I'll get off the phone."

"Colin, no, we –"

"Give me a call after your dinner, I'll update you on how my day has gone. And Flynn?"

"What?" I grunt.

"Try to have a little fun, would ya?" Colin says with a laugh before hanging up the phone.

I sigh heavily and glance down at Stella. "Okay, off the phone. You happy?"

She gives me a crooked smile. "Just want you to relax a little, Flynn. You've been on edge this whole time and…" She shrugs. "I guess you're used to going beautiful places with beautiful people."

Stella is right to point out that I seem a bit like an ingrate. Once you've been in the lap of luxury for too long, you start to get jaded. I sit on the edge of the pool and stick my legs in the water. "There. You happy?"

She laughs. "I'll take it."

I wiggle my feet back and forth. The hot sun beats against my back.

"Should I… touch you or something?" Stella asks nervously.

I feel my heart flutter. "Um. I guess."

Stella puts her hand on my knee. "Does this look awkward?"

"It feels awkward."

"Well, obviously, it feels awkward," she says, rolling her eyes. "Fine. If you want it to be weirder." Stella pushes my knees apart and steps between them looking up at me.

I can't help but notice how close she is to my crotch. Even though we're pretending, she's still a beautiful woman in between my legs. "Can I help you?"

"Yeah, fucking act like you like me," she says.

"I do like you."

She puts her elbow on my thigh and harrumphs. "Yeah, right."

I lean back on my hands. Gotta say, this is a beautiful sight. Stella has already gotten a bit of a tan from our days on the high seas and a few freckles have appeared around her nose. I swallow. Can't look for too long or else I might start feeling things I know I can't. I draw my gaze across the pool to where Adelaide is flanked by Brandy and Chiana. Her eyes are covered with round, black sunglasses that she pulls down the bridge of her nose, smirking as our eyes meet.

"Oh, shit," I whisper to myself without thinking.

Stella follows my gaze and sighs. "You're really whipped, aren't you?"

"Not whipped, just –"

"I get it. She's beautiful. But she's also an asshole," Stella says.

I laugh. "Thanks for keeping me grounded."

"Isn't that what you love about me, baby?" she taunts, batting her eyelashes up at me, her hands sliding down to my calves.

Not love, but like. Something I really like about her. Blunt, witty, and not willing to take any shit.

"I know you want to go talk to her," Stella sighs.

I almost refute her. Say I'd rather be sitting here with her.

I don't know what's true anymore.

"Take off your shirt," Stella says abruptly.

I touch the t-shirt I've been wearing since we docked. "What?"

"Come on, Flynn. Take it off," she says with a sneaking smile. "You look like a dad who is chaperoning a pool party with that thing on."

"Isn't that what I kind of am?"

"Not when you're packing those abs under there."

I raise an eyebrow.

"I share a room with you, dummy. Haven't tried to look on purpose," she says and then pushes herself off the wall, floating away. "Just saying. You might like the attention."

I watch Stella's form obscured through the water. I've been sharing a room with her too and got a few glimpses of what I shouldn't have out of the corner of my eye or reflections of the mirror. Her body is... dynamite. Nothing like that of a long, lithe model.

She's got hips and ass that don't quit no matter the time of day.

I try so hard not to look, but Stella's a knockout.

And if she thinks there's something to write home about my body too, well... I'd like to give her that satisfaction.

I pull my shirt up over my head and am immediately met with a hoot and holler from Cash and Stella.

"Stella didn't tell me you looked like that under there!" Cash cries out, nearly spilling her alcoholic slushy into the pool.

"Some things I like to keep to myself, what can I say?" Stella giggles.

I look back up to see if Adelaide has clocked it and, boy, has she ever. She's removed her sunglasses and is biting her tongue. "When did you get those, Flynn?" she asks.

Of course, she'd be surprised by them. I wasn't in such good shape back when we were together. The gym was a part of my therapy regimen. Too bad it couldn't make me forget her, only try and spite her with all my new muscles. "One... two years ago?"

Adelaide's curiosity sours, her lips pouting out. "Stella's a lucky girl."

I glance at Stella who is standing in the water with her arms folded over her chest and... she's blushing, I think. "You'd have to ask her that," I say, tilting my head back smugly. "I wouldn't want to presume."

Stella's eyes widen as she looks between Adelaide and me. "You know, I need to put more sunscreen on. Cash, can you help?"

Without another word, Stella swims to the opposite side of the pool and pushes herself out, hustling over to the lounge chair with all her beach sundries.

Cash looks over at me. "You heard her. She needs more sunscreen."

"She asked you to do it," I say.

"Are you two saving yourself for marriage or something?" Cash retorts. "Go rub some sunscreen on your girlfriend's back."

I scratch the back of my head, looking at Stella who is toweling off, and then back to Adelaide who... isn't even looking at me anymore.

In fact, she's on her feet standing with Theo, her little string bikini barely holding her in. Their fronts pressed together. They should just go find a room or have sex in the cabana if they're going to fondle each other in public.

Guess that was an easy decision.

I stand up and walk over to Stella. She's started rubbing the white lotion into her arms, taking measured breaths.

"Can I help?"

"Hm?" Stella looks up, hazel eyes wide.

"Cash told me I had to help because you're my girlfriend."

"Oh, how romantic," Stella says. She squeezes another portion of lotion onto her hand and leans down to get her legs. I purposefully look away from her so as not to stare at her ass. "Don't worry about it. I can get my back."

I grab the bottle of lotion. "Stella, let me help. I told Colin I'd take care of you. Not going to let you get burnt to a crisp."

She stands back up and puts her hands on her hips. "I'm not going to get burnt to a crisp," she snaps.

"Would you just let me put some sunscreen on your back? I'm not asking for your hand in marriage for god's sake."

Stella stares at me, pursing her lips. "Fine."

She sits on the end of the lounge with her back toward me and I sit beside her, squeezing some lotion into my palm. I rub my hands together and then eye the plane of her back. What's the best course of action to make this as quick as possible? I start at her shoulder blades and smooth my hands from the center of her back to her shoulders.

"Sorry, I'm... I just feel weird," Stella says softly.

"I know, it's a weird situation."

"I just didn't realize how much people talking about us like we're..." she lowers her voice, "...together."

I hum. "Yeah, it is a little strange." I spread the lotion down her back, digging my thumbs into her skin.

Stella giggles.

"What?"

"That... feels nice."

I smile to myself. "I've been known to give a good massage."

"Well, your next girlfriend will be very lucky."

I decide against offering to give her one later. Might sound like a come-on, even though it comes from a pure place. "I don't want you to feel stressed, Stella. All you have to do is be yourself," I murmur, getting another splat of sunscreen.

"I thought you *didn't* want me to be myself."

I push my hands onto her lower back, right above the waistband of her bikini. My mouth dries thinking about what's underneath. "I think we're both more comfortable when you're comfortable. Does that make sense?"

Stella glances over her shoulder at me. Her hazel eyes feel as though they're drawing me closer. I'm already too close. If I got any closer, our lips might meet, and I'd be done for. "Really?"

I nod. "Really, Stella." I chew on my lower lip and let my eyes fall from hers so as not to fall deeper into her spell. "Makes this feel a little more normal."

"So, you're saying I should bully you more? Would that make you feel more normal?" she teases.

"Go right ahead. It'll be like we're back in that States."

We both laugh. And before I can draw away, Stella leans into me and kisses my cheek. Her lips are so tender. Perhaps we are both more special to each other than we've previously acknowledged. After all, we share Colin, someone so special to us in completely different ways.

"What was that for?" I ask softly.

Stella shrugs. "For pretend."

I try to remember this the rest of the day when I feel my cheeks flushing when she looks my way or my nerves trembling when she's next to me.

Suddenly, this isn't feeling so pretend.

Chapter 8

Stella

I feel a gust of wind up my short dress. Tonight, I've opted to wear something Flynn bought for me. We're out at a club in Mykonos or should I say I'm *outside* a club in Mykonos. Everyone else is inside enjoying themselves in a private lounge with bottle service and mood lighting.

I feel like a fish out of water. As much as Flynn tries to make me feel comfortable or Cash compliments me, I just feel like I'm living a lie.

I guess I *technically* am. That doesn't bother me in and of itself. It's just when Adelaide or her two goons watch me, their eyes trained on me like a lion trying to catch a wildebeest, I start to feel that they can see right through me.

I'm a normie. Not famous, not special. I'm not skinny and I don't follow a diet and I don't really care if my hair gets wet or if my leg hair is a little long. It's funny how I've always been jealous of the model types. I've spent too much time in my life striving to diet or exercise my way into a size two and too much money at the salon to get my hair looking exactly the way I want it.

I feel like they see me as a woman who gave up. And maybe I did.

Maybe that's how Flynn sees me.

I am leaning up against the wall of the club, watching the line of people grow longer and longer as they wait to get inside. The air smells like salt water and cigarettes. I can't seem to shake that smell, even on the boat. Adelaide seems to go through a pack a day. How could Flynn want to kiss an ashtray?

I feel my phone buzz in my clutch and pull it out. Call from Colin. Perfect timing. "Hey," I answer quickly.

"Didn't think I'd catch you. How are you doing?"

"I've been better," I say quietly.

"Sounds busy where you are."

"Yeah, we're... we're at a club. I'm just outside because it's a little too intense for me."

Colin hesitates. "Is everything okay?"

"Yes, everything's okay. Don't be a worry wart. This is just a lot to take in." It's only been four days since I landed in Athens, yet I feel like it's been weeks away from my home.

He sighs. "Yeah, it can be."

I've stayed away from almost all of the fray of Colin's career. Colin and Flynn are considered two of the most eligible bachelors in the tech world. They're in magazines, give tons of interviews, and are talked about constantly on Twitter where everyone feels like an armchair expert. But to me, it's just my brother and his best friend. "You know there are cameras everywhere we go," I say.

"Not surprised."

"Well, someone should have warned me."

"Don't hold that against Flynn. They're part and parcel to our lives now. He's way more used to it than me, though. I mean he dealt with Adelaide and her constant swarm of paparazzi for way longer than I would have been able to."

I look down the cobblestone road at a black van that I've noticed following us at most of our locations. There are at least three photographers who are camped out in there. They must have taken a ferry from Santorini in order to follow us. How they knew where we'd be going, I can only guess.

Friends of the rich and famous aren't always so *friendly*.

"Well, just know if I'm ever in a picture holding hands with Flynn or something it's not real."

Colin laughs, "I know that. I'm surprised you're even letting him hold your hand."

"Yeah, me too." Four days ago we were squabbling on the dock in Athens. Now, we're holding hands in public. We might be acting, but I can't ignore what it's been doing to my insides. Mush, right away. And sleeping next to him the past few nights has been… nice. I haven't slept beside anyone except my dogs in a couple of years. Which reminds me… "How's Freckles?"

"She's good. She won't eat the dry food, though."

Colin has been watching Freckles. I hate to give her separation anxiety right away, but I'm happy to know my little senior dog has a home with Flynn when he returns.

"Stella…"

"What?"

"You're stalling. Just go back inside, have a couple of shots, and enjoy yourself. This is a vacation," Colin reprimands.

Is it though? To be on edge at all moments pretending to be Flynn's girlfriend while quietly nursing the littlest nugget of a romantic attraction to him? *Relax, Stella. If you spent this much time with any man, you'd probably be in love with him.* I need to get back on the apps once I get home. I've been single for too long. "Okay, fine."

"You just text me if you need a boost, alright?"

"Love you, Col."

"You too, Stell. Bye."

I hang up and slip my phone back into my clutch. Take a deep breath of the warm Mykonos air, and bask in the starry night.

"Hey, I've been looking for you."

I turn to find Flynn poking his head out of the door of the club. He's looking absolutely *fine* tonight. Light blue linen shirt unbuttoned just enough to start giving me a peek at that beautiful chest and a pair of khakis. And, of course, he's wearing his glasses which is just *adorable*.

And he was looking for me. That counts for something.

"Yeah, just needed some fresh air," I say, taking a few steps toward him.

"The cigarette smoke will do that," Flynn replies with a grin. He takes a step closer to me. "We can go back to the boat if you're not having fun."

I quirk my lips to the side. "Who says I'm not having fun?"

He shrugs. "No one. But since you snuck off, I had to wonder if –"

"Flynn! Flynn! Over here!"

I leap into the air at the sound of a camera flashing. Flynn grabs me by the arm just as I get a glimpse at one of the paparazzi. They must have been waiting for something like this to happen.

"Who is your lady friend?! Give her a kiss!"

"Have a nice night, gentleman," Flynn says, shuffling me into the buoyant, bouncing club before anyone can say another word. He puts his hand on the nape of my neck. "You okay?"

Better now. "Yeah, I'm fine."

Flynn's hand slides down my back, but just before he can withdraw entirely, I grab his hand. "Let's do shots."

"What?"

"I need to loosen up. And I can't do shots alone," I say, trying not to sound like I'm begging. "That'd be embarrassing, right?"

Flynn concedes with a nod. "Suppose you're right." Then he smiles. "Okay. Let's do shots."

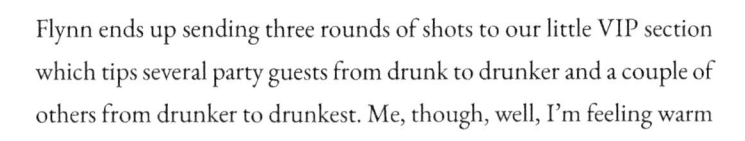

Flynn ends up sending three rounds of shots to our little VIP section which tips several party guests from drunk to drunker and a couple of others from drunker to drunkest. Me, though, well, I'm feeling warm and wonderful.

"Stella, Stella, Stella." Cash grabs onto my arm. "Gregory and I are going dancing."

"Oh, you don't want me to get in your way," I say. I've been sitting next to Flynn since we returned, and I'd hate to leave the warmth of his hip pressed up to mine. More than that, I'd hate to leave Flynn alone with Adelaide and Theo. Half of me worries about what she'll do and the other half worries about what *he'll* do. "Besides, we're..." I glance at Flynn, not sure what to say to finish that sentence.

Flynn cracks a smile. The alcohol has seeped in along his brow. He's usually so serious and stern. Now, he's at ease. "Don't worry about me. You go have fun."

Without another word, Cash pulls me up off the sofa with more strength than a woman of her stature should have. "Come on! Daddy said you can come out to play! Let's go!"

Cash, Gregory, and I wade out of the safety of the VIP area onto the dance floor. I glance back at Flynn who gives me a big thumbs up. Inside, I cringe. That's not a gesture you make to a girl you might be attracted to.

Not that he should be attracted to me. But I'll admit, it would be nice.

Adelaide and her friends can't be as freewheeling since they're so recognizable. Plus, I bet Theo's a better dancer than her. I asked him if footballers really take ballet, and he said it was his favorite part of the job.

Theo is an interesting man; I can say that much.

Over the loudspeakers is some pop song mashed together with different thumping and squealing sounds. The DJ up front is *feeling* the music with everything in her. I've heard her name before but wouldn't know the first thing about famous DJs.

The three of us start dancing in a triangle, making a spot for ourselves among the other wasted clubbers. I start to lose myself in the music, putting my hands in the air and wriggling my hips in time to the beat. Cash and Gregory sing the lyrics and I suddenly recognize the song too, singing along with them. The alcohol completely did the trick.

This feels like freedom.

From time to time, I look back at Flynn, waiting to be disappointed to see him talking to Adelaide. But every time his eyes are squarely on me.

Thank goodness too. After not too long, I feel a hand slink around my hip. Some tall bastard with a grip like Rocky Balboa pulls me up against his crotch. I look at him with disgust, but he seems very pleased with himself. "What, you don't want to dance with me?"

"No," I say angrily and try to pull away.

"You play hard to get, then?"

"I'm not playing at all." I smack him on the chest. "Let me go, let me –"

"Hey man, she's with me" I hear Flynn's voice over the music.

The man releases his grip on me, and I trip back into Flynn's chest. Flynn wraps his arm around my waist protectively.

"Sorry, sorry. Forgive me," the stranger says, holding his hands up in the air. He's not speaking to me but to Flynn. Fury bubbles inside of me.

Flynn doesn't say anything else, moving in between me and the man. "Are you okay?"

"God, what a fucking jackass," I say. "Of course, he won't listen to me, but the second a man steps in –"

"Hey."

I stop speaking and look up at Flynn in surprise. It was a very emphatic "hey".

"You were having fun," he says. "You should keep having fun."

He's right. *Fuck* that guy. I'm going to keep having a good time. I grab Flynn's hands, looking up into his blue eyes. "Dance with me?"

Flynn laughs, his voice cracking. "I'm a bad dancer."

"Everyone's drunk. We're all bad dancers," I reply and grab his hand. "Please? Would make me feel safer." It's only a half-truth. It would make me feel safer.

But it's not why I want him to dance with me.

Flynn looks around the club and puffs up his chest. "Okay."

I smile and put his hand on my waist. His touch is electric. Or maybe it's the tequila. Whatever it is, it feels amazing. "Just follow my lead."

He chuckles. "I can do that."

And he does. All it takes is a couple of seconds to get into the groove of the music before the two of us are working the floor, closer and closer until our chests are pressed together. Flynn isn't as bad as he'd warned me. In fact, once he gets out of his head, he's got a few steps in him, spinning me around and gyrating his hips.

We laugh as we weave in and out of each other on the floor. I forget about everyone else. It's just me and Flynn and our fake relationship that's starting to feel a crumb more real every moment.

Flynn grabs my hand. "I'm gonna spin you out, ready?"

"Oh god, I might fall!" I cry out, but it's too late. He flicks me out away from him and I spin out onto the floor, nearly tripping over my own feet. Flynn's grip is tight and sure, though. He swings me right back into him so my back is up against his chest and...

I can feel him through his pants, a slight bulge at my back. Is this for real? Is he...turned on?

"What am I going to do with you, Stella?" he asks, hot tequila breath on my face.

I tilt my head back. Seem obvious what comes next. "I think you know."

And then he kisses me.

Flynn Madden kisses me.

And not just a kiss for show. A real kiss. A kiss that says, "I want more."

For once he didn't question me. Didn't argue with me. He just did it.

I slide my hand around the back of his head, drawing him further into me.

Fuck it. If he's my fake boyfriend, then I'm going to act like it.

Consequences be damned.

Chapter 9

Flynn

I blink my eyes open to find a mess of brown curls crowding my vision. Somehow, my vision is perfectly clear. I must have slept in my glasses. My head pounds. God, what happened last night?

I take a deep breath and get an inhale of that hair. Smells like fruity shampoo, cigarettes, and... tequila.

The memory of last night hits me all at once. I shudder away from the scent and leap out of bed. Damn any unfolding hangover, I need to get as far away from that smell as possible. I stare down at Stella in the bed next to me. Her limbs are flung in different directions and she's snorting lightly, mouth hanging open.

I touch my chest. I still have my shirt on. I move my hand a little lower... still have my pants on. Thank God. I can't imagine if anything had happened, I would have had the wherewithal to put my trousers back on.

Then, my lips tingle.

We may not have had sex, but we certainly kissed. In fact, I remember kissing *a lot*. Even one kiss is one too many. Stella Banks is *totally* off-limits.

Stella flips over onto her belly into the spot I left in bed and lets out a long, sleepy sigh. I hold my breath for what feels like a whole minute, waiting to see if she's still asleep.

I tiptoe into the bathroom and slide the door closed.

Get yourself together, Madden. I turn on the faucet and splash some water on my face, relieving some of the pain in my head if only for a moment.

I stare at my reflection in the mirror. God, I look like a wreck. My hair is all pushed to one side, my shirt mussed, and my skin looks sallow from the alcohol. My eyes flick to a spot on my neck, dark and purple. Is that…is that a hickey?

I touch it carefully and wince. Yep. That's a hickey. Things really got out of hand last night.

My stomach flips and nausea creeps in. Not only am I hungover, but I'm on a boat hungover. That's a combination for losing my lunch if I ever heard one.

"Flynn?" I hear Stella call out in a weak voice.

"Yeah, I'm in here, I'm…" I slide the bathroom door back open and find Stella sitting up in bed rubbing her eyes. I have to suck in a tight breath. Stella looks gorgeous, all crinkly with slumber. "Morning."

"What time is it?" she asks, massaging her forehead. "God, my head."

"Not sure, I just got up," I say. "And have no idea where my phone is."

Stella drops her hands, the strap of her silvery mini dress falling off her shoulder, nearly exposing her chest to me. "I don't remember getting back on the boat last night."

"Me either," I say, retracing my steps through the tiny cabin for my phone.

"Oh god, did we –"

"No!" I say, all too aggressively. "I mean we did but we didn't."

Stella furrows her brow. "What's that mean?" Then, her eyes widen. "What happened to your neck?"

That kiss must have unlocked something in me because I can't even look at her now without fearing I might get hard. I focus harder on finding my phone, tossing one of the blankets aside to find it twirled up in a sheet. "You happened to it, I think," I mutter, checking the time. "Nearly eleven."

Stella's shoulders drop. "Oh god, Flynn, I'm sorry."

I swallow. I wish she wouldn't apologize. It probably shouldn't have happened but that doesn't mean I didn't enjoy it. "Don't apologize. It was – I was there too."

"Right, of course, just... I should have known what tequila would do to me."

It's clear she regrets it. And that hurts more than I'd like it to. "Listen, we were both drunk, sometimes it just happens. I think we can both agree on that."

"Yeah, of course. *Of course*," Stella says.

I can't stand in this small cabin with her looking all bed-flushed and beautiful. I can practically smell her from here and it's getting hard to resist these feelings that have been building in me.

"Let's just pretend it didn't happen," Stella murmurs softly.

How the hell am I supposed to do that? "Agreed. It was a mistake," I reply though I don't mean it.

It's as if all the closeness we've built in this short time disappears into thin air. Back to begrudging pretend lovers.

"We've got a sea day today and half of tomorrow, so let's just try and take some space," Stella says, pulling the blankets up over her chest as if she's naked.

I feel my cheeks burning with heat, my stomach starting to twist not just from the leftover alcohol, but shame. I can't believe I was so dumb as to kiss her. More than that, I can't believe I let myself want her.

"I need some air," I say and leave the cabin without another word. I don't just need some air. I need a cold plunge in the ocean or a slap in the face.

I need to get as far as possible from Stella as possible.

"Beers!" Theo shouts, cracking open the cooler.

I've joined the guys out on the tender for a day of fishing which apparently was just a guise for us all to get obnoxiously drunk in the middle of the ocean. I'm definitely the odd man out. Everyone else is a sportsman. You've got Theo, of course, and then his teammates, Will and Franklin who look like they could each pull a freight train. And then his friend Simon who is a player for Manchester United. He's much more my type of guy framewise, but he's all soccer up in the head.

Surprisingly, Gregory also joined us. In fact, he's the only one fishing. I guess I shouldn't have assumed the gay guy would want to hang back with the girls. Turns out, he grew up in the Pacific Northwest and spent lots of time on his father's boat pulling in halibut the size of a sow. He tried to show me his technique earlier, but I ended up snapping my line trying to pull in a piece of driftwood.

I gave up after that. Might as well drink my problems away.

"Your neck is lookin' better today, Flynn," Theo says, pointing to his own vascular neck, before throwing me a beer.

I nearly lose it over the edge of the tender, the metal slipping through my fingers and into my lap. "Thanks," I grumble.

"For a man sharing a bed with a beautiful woman, you sure are a grumpy Gus, aren't you?" Simon says in his spry British accent.

I glare at him.

"Uh-oh, trouble in paradise, huh?" Theo says, thwapping one of his bros on the chest.

I sigh. "Something like that." Since leaving the cabin yesterday morning, Stella and I haven't said more than a few words to each other. Even at dinner last night we barely shared a glance. I spent most of yesterday on the deck, hurling my guts out over the side of the boat as we plowed through the beautiful Med waters. So, this morning, when Adelaide suggested that once we anchored the boys and girls should split for the day, I jumped at the chance. Who cares if they're all meatheads? Better than having to avoid Stella all day.

"Growing pains, eh?" Simon asks with a jolly grin.

"How do you mean?"

Simon shrugs. "You know. The plateaus of a relationship."

I open my beer and take a thoughtful sip. I would say that Stella and I are in the exact opposite of a plateau. It's more like a volcano is heating up, feels close to exploding. "I guess things are feeling a little stilted."

"Well, how long have you been together?"

Get the facts straight, don't blow your cover. "Five months, plus a little extra."

"But you've known each other a while, right? Adelaide says you work with her brother," Theo says, kicking his feet up on one of the seats.

"Yes, I've known her for..." Here goes the mental math. "Gosh fourteen years, I guess?"

The guys all exchange looks.

"What's that look for?"

"Have things moved fast?" Will continues the questioning.

You could say that. "Yeah, I guess."

"And you're just now putting a label on things? Yeesh, brother," Franklin says which receives laughter from the other guys.

"What's wrong with that?" I don't know why I'm indulging in this. It's not even a real relationship. I guess I'm just interested to hear how it looks from the outside. Let me know if we're doing a good job of faking it.

"Well, when you have a history, girls expect you to move faster," Franklin continues.

"She's a woman, not a girl," Gregory shouts out from his place at the back of the boat. He looks like a real fisherman with his rod and bucket hat.

"*Women* expect you to move faster. Because you don't have to get through all the bullshit of getting to know each other."

I chuckle. "I guess, although Stella and I didn't much like each other before…"

"Ooo enemies to lovers," Simon says, twiddling his fingers.

I give him a look.

"Simon loves romance novels," Theo answers my confusion. "Listen, I'm sure there's like a huge microscope on you guys right now. Celebrating an engagement, making your public debut. That's a lot of pressure."

I'm shocked that the man who gets shocked in the head for a living has a lot of thoughtful points about love and romance.

Maybe that's what Adelaide likes so much about him. He's got a head for romance and love. I wasn't ever able to do that for her. I was so concerned with Wired Reality and everything my company needed. Past the honeymoon stage, I think I took her for granted as someone who would always be there. Then she wasn't.

I think if I got another chance *now,* I'd be a great boyfriend.

Perhaps not for Adelaide. Maybe... someone else.

Not naming names, though.

"Well, you guys have seen us together. What do you think we're missing?" I ask somewhat genuinely.

"I wasn't sure you two had chemistry until you were dancing the other night," Will says.

"Oh, you'd have to be a ninny not to see that chemistry," Simon tsks. "I saw it well before then."

Theo takes a swig of his beer and looks up into the hot Mediterranean sun as if he's a philosopher about to bestow the biggest kernel of wisdom ever bestowed. "I think you respect her too much."

I gape. "I'm sorry?"

"That sounded bad, Tee," Franklin whispers.

"Let me explain, alright, don't get your jockstrap in a bunch," Theo replies, spreading his arms out to take the floor. "What I mean to say is you've spent a lot of time being her friend –"

Friend might be a stretch.

"And now, you're concerned you're going to hurt her. You're not willing to take risks. Tell me if that feels familiar."

I nod slowly. "Yeah. You're right."

"So, you gotta take some risks!" Theo exclaims and slaps my thigh.

I have to say, Theo's a good guy. I've always made him a villain in my head. But to allow your fiancé's ex to come to your engagement party and to treat him like a friend... that takes a lot of courage I don't think I have.

"Show her how you really feel about her. Unbutton one more button on your shirt and show her what kind of man you are."

I can't believe he's starting to make sense. Fuck this dancing around each other, too afraid to talk.

I want Stella. And I need her to know that.

"Go on. Do it," Theo encourages.

I look down at my shirt and carefully unbutton the next button. It's a bit exposing for me; I've always ascribed this look to seventies rock stars and flamboyant guys visiting Fire Island.

The guys all hoot and holler. "There ya go, Madden!" Simon gleefully shouts, slapping me on the back.

Suddenly, the boat lurches backward and Gregory shouts, "Guys! A little help!" He's struggling to reel in a fish, the rod bending further and further toward the water.

"Alright, guys," Theo announces, leaping up. "Let's do this."

The other guys all run to help Gregory. I'd just get in the way so I stay put.

Besides, I've got to prepare to show Stella what kind of man I really am.

Chapter 10

Stella

I have been staring out at the water, desperate to see the tender on the horizon. I might not be speaking to Flynn at this moment in time, but he's the only thing I have out here. My only source of comfort.

Among other things.

I should have known better than to get drunk the other night. I knew that could only lead to me making a fool of myself. I just didn't count on Flynn being willing to make a fool of himself with me.

"What are you looking at out there, girlie?" Cash asks, leaning on the arm of my chair.

"Uhm, I –" I quickly look back to the group of girls. We're all sitting around with our toes drying from a pedicure, sipping mimosas. "They've been out there a while. I just hope Flynn's putting on his sunscreen."

"Oh, yeah," Adelaide giggles. "He just burns, doesn't he?"

It's silly for me to feel possessive over a man who isn't mine to begin with. But if he's not mine he's *certainly* not hers. After all, I'm the one sleeping next to him. And kissing him. And *marking* him. I've had to hide a smile every time someone points it out. "Yes, I'd hate for him to be in misery with a sunburn," I say to her, forcing a smile. Then I look down at my toes. I picked a turquoise blue. Feels very juvenile when I compare them with all the other girls who picked various shades of beige.

"Flynn's going to be miserable no matter what," Adelaide scoffs.

I eye her across the circle. "What's that mean?"

She shrugs, sipping on her mimosa. She loves to play dumb after saying the most heinous shit.

"No, really," I egg her on with an innocent smile. "You think he's miserable?"

"Well, not with you. That's obvious, girl," she smiles back at me with a cattishness that puts me on edge. "Just when we were together, he was always working and, well, the poor thing didn't really know how to enjoy himself. I just hope he's figured that out since."

"Right, well it's been two years. He's had a lot of time to grow, don't you think?" I ask, returning her condescending lilt back to her like this is a game of tennis.

Adelaide's green eyes sharpen in mine. "His taste has certainly changed, I'll say that."

"Oh, Adelaide, don't be a bitch," Cash interrupts, touching my arm. "Just because Flynn wasn't the guy you wanted him to be doesn't mean he isn't good for someone else."

"I know that, Cash," Adelaide replies with some bitterness, flicking her blonde hair over her shoulder. "We're just different types of girls. I think Stella would agree with that."

This is what I was afraid of. Not just feeling othered but *being* othered. Women like Adelaide know how to wield their looks like swords. And, man, does it cut deep. I manage my last scrap of dignity and nod, "We are. Very different."

"I think what Adelaide means is that, you know, you're like a regular girl," Brandy peeps up in her southern twang. She says the word regular as if it's some exotic thing. You know, you're normal. I think I'm a little jealous. Aren't you a little jealous, Addy?"

I shake my head. "We don't have to do this. You know?" I try to laugh it off. "Like, we all know I'm not famous or rich. I'm just along for the ride."

"Well, you will be famous and rich as long as you're with Flynn," Adelaide says, her voice low and dry.

"What are you implying?"

Adelaide eyes me. She takes a long sip of her mimosa. Then, she licks her top teeth. "I'm just saying I wouldn't blame you if that was a big part of why you're together. I know how difficult he can be."

She's questioning my character. But that's not even why I'm mad. I'm with Flynn because this is a business transaction. Fuck whatever she thinks about why I'm here. I'm mad because she's talking about Flynn as if he's some corporate robot. Admittedly, I've seen him that way in the past, probably even called him that in an argument.

Even so. That's *my* corporate robot. Not hers.

"I'm not going to sit here and tell you that the experience you had in a relationship with Flynn isn't true. But I'd thank you for not assuming that I've had the same experience. It's been two years after all. You've both grown," I say, feeling satisfied that I've put the kibosh on the conversation.

Adelaide sighs. "I'd agree with you, but he did come to my party, didn't he? Didn't grow *that* much."

"*Adelaide*," Cash snaps.

My heart is chasing itself in a circle. Flynn has been hung up on her since the breakup and he did enlist me to fake a relationship with him in order to show her he's moved on. Or make her jealous. So why am I letting myself believe anything is growing between us? Not only can it never happen. It won't. I'm here as a conduit. Not a lover.

I'm not here for love or to defend Flynn. All I am is a prop. A tool. At least now I can say a supermodel has broken my heart.

"I think my toes are dry," I say, getting to my feet. "I'm going to go rest before dinner."

"Stella, don't go, it's –" Cash pulls on the skirt of my coverup, but I ignore it and keep on walking.

I hurry down the steps to the lower decks, stopping only to pull the spacers out from between my toes. Once I'm in my cabin, I throw myself onto the bed and burst into tears.

What the hell is happening to me? We're a day short of one week on this godforsaken trip and my whole world has been turned upside down. No one told me that the Mediterranean air was an intoxicant. I feel like I've been drunk since the moment I found Flynn on the dock.

We're both too good at pretending. The intertwined arms, hand holding, intimate touches. You can't *fake* those. Only the feeling behind them. And I've never been good at faking my feelings.

I think a sliver of this has been here all along. From the moment I met Flynn, he was my brother's best friend. Forbidden. So, I leaned into my disdain, and pushed him away harder and harder, like a rubber band growing taut the further you pull it.

It was inevitable that it would snap back with viciousness.

Now here I am.

Alone off the coast of Corfu, falling for my brother's best friend while he continues to pine for his ex-girlfriend.

I'm completely pathetic.

My wallowing is interrupted by a flurry of feet above me and loud shouts and greetings. The boys' group must have returned. I close my eyes tightly. *Fuck*. Flynn will probably want the room for a nap and I'll have to go back out there and deal with... *them*.

I push myself up out of bed and go into the bathroom. *Wipe away the tears.* This is all for a good cause. Just another week and then I'll be back home. The shelter will have a fatter checkbook, Freckles will have a home, and Flynn and I will never have to speak of this again.

Fuck, pretending nothing has happened is tearing me apart.

I hear Flynn rap at the door. "Stella? Are you decent?"

"Shit," I whisper to myself and try to straighten myself out. "Just a second!" I call out. I adjust the front of my coverup and smooth my hair, twisting my fingers through the curls. *Deep breath.* "Okay, you can come in."

I hear the door open and force myself not to peek out of the bathroom to look at Flynn. I don't want to see his sun-kissed skin and blue eyes somehow tinted bluer from the sea. That just might give me a heart attack. "How was fishing?"

"Good, Gregory caught something," he says.

"Really? That's amazing," I say, feigning a good attitude. He doesn't need to know that Adelaide was attacking me. Then I'd have to tell him what she said about him. I don't know if Flynn could handle it.

I hear his boat shoes pad closer to the bathroom. "How was it here?"

"Um. Good. Got a pedicure. You want to see?" I ask.

Flynn chuckles. "Sure."

Before I can step out of the bathroom, Flynn steps into the doorframe and leans against it with his forearm. Fuck, he's tall, but the low ceiling makes him look even taller. He smells like coconut sunscreen and sweat. *Delicious.* And his shirt... holy shit, it's like halfway unbuttoned, revealing more of his chest than I've seen in a couple of days.

"Blue! Nice," he says.

Right, he's looking at my toes. I glance down at my feet. "Yeah, turquoise."

"Oh, sorry, turquoise," he replies.

I look at him hesitantly. Why does he have to stand so close? "Yeah, you know, I like to teach you a thing or two every now and then," I say with a half-smile.

Flynn's smile fades. I hear him gulp, his Adam's apple bobbing. His blue eyes fall from mine. "Were the girls okay?"

"Oh, yeah. They were fine. I don't know if they like me but yeah, they were fine." I give a final sigh. "Could you move?"

"What?"

"I'd like to leave the bathroom?" I say, suddenly feeling claustrophobic from how he's looming in the doorway.

Flynn swallows hard. It's... stirring. Is that weird? It does something to me. "Um, I... I can't do that."

I'm not even paying attention to what he's saying. His voice is low and luscious. Only for me. I want to wrap myself up in that voice like it's a blanket. Stay awhile, cozy up, and let it envelop every part of me.

Oh no.

"Because if I do, I'll lose my nerve."

Lose his nerve? What's he talking about? Unless...

Suddenly, I realize just how close we are. I haven't been able to ignore that since we've arrived. In our tiny room, sitting side by side at dinner, having to walk hand in hand. I've been bristling away from it every moment, even after our kiss (especially after our kiss). Now, though, his blushed lips are right there, his scent of sweat and coconut is fucking divine, and I can feel my body not wanting to resist him any longer.

Which is why when he leans down and kisses me, I don't resist. He grabs my bicep and pulls me toward him, so we are chest to chest. I slide my arm around his neck, pulling myself onto my tiptoes, making sure he knows that not only am I right here with him in this, but also that I'm not going anywhere.

Because now that he's crossed this line, he's unleashed something in me.

"Stella…" he whispers between my lips.

There's no time for idle talk. I kiss him again, harder, my tongue diving between his lips. I taste ouzo and desperation and, God, he's a good kisser. I was too drunk to know the last time, but now I can truly measure every sensation. The way his lips caress mine is going to be hard to forget.

I have to make this count.

I throw myself into Flynn's arms; he stumbles back, nearly falling. Instead, we crash onto the bed a flurry of arms, legs, and lips. I pop my head up and touch his chest. "Are you okay?"

"Yeah, yeah, I'm fine," he nods eagerly.

I touch his chest carefully. "Sorry, I got a little carried away, I…"

My eyes meet his and I lose my train of thought. Flynn's lips perk into a tiny smile as if to say, *Don't be sorry.*

I spread my hands wider across his pecks and shake my head. "What are we doing?"

"I think you know."

"We can't."

"I know."

I close my eyes, gripping the front of his shirt. "Flynn, what am I supposed to do?"

He chuckles. "What do you mean?"

"You know what I mean!"

We are both silent for a second. I drop my forehead down to his chest. I want to kiss it so bad…

Flynn grabs my wrist and leads it carefully down further and further until we're at the point of no return. My fingers brush over his groin. Then, he settles my hand against him over his hardened length.

Holy shit, he's huge.

"Stella, I need you."

My eyes snap back to his. Oh god, the look in his eye is so full of need. Blue eyes trembling like the sea before a storm.

He continues through clenched teeth. "Need you so bad, it's…"

Who am I to deny a man this desperate? Especially when I can feel my center trembling for him already. I squeeze his cock in my hand through the front of his shorts. Flynn winces, pushing his head back into the comforter and gasping.

No more talking, Stella. Action.

We both want it. It's obvious. Forget everything else.

I need to fuck him.

Our lips collide once again as I position my hips over his. I undulate my hips, pressing his hardness against my panties. It's revving me up, getting me wetter and wetter.

Flynn's hands slide down my back, lower and lower, until he's reached my backside. Carefully, he scrunches the fabric of my sun dress up over my ass until he can feel it with his bare hands. He moans into my mouth. "Fuck, Stella, you feel so good."

I'm glad we're so close together that he can't see me blush. It's been a long time since I've been in bed with a man, and I've forgotten how it feels to be worshipped.

"So fucking beautiful," he whispers, moving his mouth into the crook of my neck. He begins to kiss it ravenously. I can feel his teeth nipping at my neck. *Payback,* I think and begin to laugh.

Abruptly, Flynn flips me onto the bed, my wrists trapped under his hands. But his lips don't break away, not for a second.

I cry out in surprise, relishing his weight on top of mine.

He lifts his mouth from my neck, lips parted.

We both breathe heavily as our eyes are locked. I can feel him, a hundred percent man, laboring against my clothed entrance.

"I want to fuck you so bad, Stella," Flynn says in a wanting voice like I've never heard. An animal that needs to be released.

I wiggle my hips under him. "Do it."

He takes a deep breath, chest puffing outward, pushing himself up to his knees between my legs. "I want to see you," he adds softly.

Now I know I'm blushing, but there's no point in being self-conscious at this point. As Flynn takes off his shirt, I pull my dress over my head and toss it behind me, leaving me in nothing but my underwear. I've never been one for bras. They make my back hurt. And they make moments like this much easier.

Flynn has paused in his own disrobing, staring at my chest. He shakes his head, smiling. "Fuck."

"What?"

"You know what."

I laugh hard. I *do* know what because I feel the exact same way about him. His chest is beautiful. Not overly worked, but toned just enough that he looks strong with a spattering of virile hair across his pecs and trailing down from his belly button.

Flynn starts to undo his shorts, but I have other things in mind. "Wait. Let me." I sit up between his legs and push his hands away from the waistband. Carefully, slowly, I undo the closure and kiss the spot right at the base of his sternum. His skin is covered in goosebumps. Then, I look up at him tucking my chin against his front just as I push his shorts down. They fall to the ground. I can feel his cock loll against my breast. If I wasn't desperate to have him inside, I would swallow him up without hesitation.

Flynn cups the back of my head in his hand, fingers looping through my curls.

"Your turn," I whisper before reclining back on the bed.

Flynn hums and hooks his fingers around the waistband of my panties. As he works them down, my hips rise off the bed, out of my control. Wanting. This is perfect for his purposes because the second my panties fly off my ankle, he's pushed himself up in between my thighs, sliding his cock through my juicy center. "Mmm, you're so warm."

We kiss softly as he explores my folds. As desperate as I feel, I want him to feel taken care of. He's not just a man I met in Greece. He's Colin's best friend. He's a part of my life.

If we have to go back and pretend like this never happened, at least we can have memories filled with tenderness.

The head of Flynn's cock nudges my entrance. "Is this okay…?"

I nod. "Yes, please."

His eyes lock in mine as he sinks into me. The eye contact makes the feeling of him stretching me even more intense. My mouth drops open with trembling breath.

"Oh god," he mutters, shutting his eyes. "Feels so good."

I slide my hands down his back. "You got it, baby. Just like that."

Further and further, he sinks until most of Flynn is inside me.

Oh my god. Flynn is inside me. And it feels amazing.

We could stay just like this and I'd be satisfied. But we both know that's not what's happening.

Flynn starts to slide in and out of me at a slow tempo, trying to steady his breath and failing. The fact I'm making him feel so good makes me feel amazing. Combine that with how his length and width are brushing up against my g-spot every time he enters me, I know I'm not long for this fight.

I slide my hands up his back and dig my fingernails into his shoulder blades. "God, you're so big."

"Am I hurting you?"

"No, no, it's amazing. Keep going. Harder."

Flynn nods, a lock of his brown hair falling onto his forehead. He bucks his hips faster.

I grab the back of his head and kiss him, our lips landing in peculiar, needy combinations that send me into overdrive. Suddenly, my legs are shaking and I'm plowing my hips in tandem with his. Flynn groans into my mouth. I'm about to wrap my hands around his ass and help him drive into me with some leverage, but he has other things in mind. He pulls me onto his knees and fucks me with my lower back on the flats of his thighs. At this new angle, I can't help but cry out.

"God, those sounds," he says, shaking his head. "You're going to make me come from those sounds, Stella."

My head rolls back on the bed as I grab onto the comforter on either side of my head. Flynn has his hands glued to my hips, driving his length harder and faster. The world is starting to spin, a fire burning in my belly. "Fuck me, fuck me, fuck me," I whimper. "I'm so close."

A wild look passes through Flynn's eyes and somehow, he drives even faster into me. I moan, the sound trembling with every thrust. "Wait for me," he grunts.

If I can, I will.

Because I don't just want him to come. I want him to come in me. Even though I'm on the pill, I usually take more precautions than this. But I can't help it.

I need every bit.

"Oh my god," I whimper, latching my hands onto his. "Flynn, please."

"You take me so good, baby. You're taking all of me."

"I'm so… I'm so… I'm –" My eyes roll back as the heat rips up through me, and the orgasm sends my body spasming.

All it takes is the tightening of my pussy for Flynn to join me. He jerks, slams his cock into me once more, and then releases, a growl emanating from his mouth and echoing through the room. I can feel every bit of his hot seed flooding into me, extending my orgasm even longer. I grab for something, anything, my hand landing against his forearm.

"It's okay," I hear him whisper. "Let it all go."

My mouth drops open, and I let out a final moan. I haven't felt this good in a long time. Maybe ever.

Flynn's hips jerk into me by accident. "Shit, sorry, I…"

"It's okay," I say, but barely. My mouth is so dry from panting that I can barely speak.

Flynn slides out of me and then folds himself over me, kissing me with all the gentleness he can muster, right on my lips. "Stella, you're amazing," he whispers.

I giggle, wrapping my arms around his back, playing with the small trail of hair at the base of his skull. "What are you talking about? I didn't do anything. You're the amazing one."

"Well…" Flynn trails off and draws me into his arms so my head is resting on his chest. "Let's just say we were both amazing."

I kiss his chest and feel his heart racing right against my lips. "Maybe we were." I resist telling him no man has ever made me feel this good in my life. I don't want to look desperate and certainly don't want to give him the impression I have hopes this might continue once we're back in the States.

"Would you do that again with me sometime?" he asks in a voice so quiet it's almost like he didn't want me to hear.

Though I know I should deny him, that we should cut this off at the neck before we're in over our heads, I can't help myself. "Absolutely."

The rest of this trip is going to be a fucking blast.

Chapter 11

Flynn

When one of the stews approached me this morning and asked if I'd like to take my "girlfriend' on an excursion, I was taken aback.

Apparently, she could sense my shock. "I beg your pardon if I'm intruding. You two just seemed to be so in love last night, and I couldn't help but think you might want some time apart from the rest of the group," she explained.

I was damn near speechless. "In love"? Maybe she was too pure at heart to notice the difference between the afterglow of sex versus the big L word, but...

Love?

Despite my logical side wanting to dismiss her offer, I couldn't help but be curious. "What'd you have in mind?"

This is how Stella and I ended up alone on this tender driven by one of the crew members, a tall American guy from Idaho named Trent, a picnic basket firmly between us on the seat.

"Where did you say we were going?" Stella asks as the tender starts to slow down as we approach a rocky outcrop.

"She said there was some grotto... I don't know, I kinda just left all the planning to her," I reply nervously.

We share a glance that I quickly look away from. It's been damn near impossible for me to stop staring. Stella's beauty is suddenly as prominent as the Mediterranean sun to me. I don't know how I didn't see it before. From her mop of brown curls piled on her head to her flushed freckled cheeks to her elegant collar bone to... well, everything else. If eyes could eat, mine would be overstuffed.

"Didn't know you could be so shy, Flynn," she remarks in a low voice.

I feel a zip of electricity up my back. "I'm not shy!"

"Really? Is that why you keep looking away from me? As if we didn't..." Stella cocks her eyebrow upward. "Three times yesterday?"

Yes, it wasn't just once before dinner. It was twice before dinner. And once after.

This doesn't even include our encounter we had first thing this morning between the sheets, our eyes barely open.

Beyond her quirky exterior, Stella is a goddess in the bedroom. A sheer marvel. And I have a whole 'nother week to enjoy her before...

Well, let's not think about going home. Let's just enjoy the present.

"I can't help it. You make me nervous," I mutter softly.

"Me? Your sworn enemy?"

I laugh. "Not my sworn enemy."

"Sure, whatever you say, Flynn." Stella reaches over the basket and kisses me lightly on the lips.

Doesn't matter if her touch is passionate or gentle. It sends sparks through every inch of my body whenever she touches me. I sigh, "God, what am I going to do with you?"

"I have many ideas," she smirks.

"Alright! We're coming up on the grotto right up ahead!" the first mate announces, pointing up ahead at a bend in the blue water.

I'd been so caught up in Stella I didn't even notice how the boat had slipped in between two cliff sides, leading us further and further into a maze of rocks.

Shortly after, just as promised, a grotto, the water so clear you can see the bottom. The sun is just enough out of the way that the light is indirect, cooling down the hot Med air immensely.

"Wow..." Stella says, looking over the edge of the boat.

The grotto is edged in on three sides, with a large floating dock anchored in the center, and a very small rocky plateau against the north wall.

The tender edges up to the dock. Trent leaps out and helps us onto the dock along with the picnic basket. "I'll be back in two hours. If you need anything, I'll leave a com with you."

"Thanks, Trent," I say with a curt nod.

The cheerful younger man leaps back into the tender and drives off. His departure feels as slow as molasses. I want Stella all to myself. The sooner, the better.

"Ooo! Brie!" Stella chirps.

I turn around to find she's already broken into the picnic basket. I was hoping to get in a quickie before our bellies were full, but... that's fine. "If you want to swim, you should do that first."

"Or what, the leeches will get me?"

"You might get a cramp and we're all alone out here. I'd have to save you."

Stella scoffs. "Fine." She gets back to her feet and pulls her cover-up over her head, revealing a sleek black bikini.

I gulp. "I haven't seen you wear that before."

She laughs. "Cash let me borrow it. When she heard we were going out, she was all like, 'You can't wear that stodgy one-piece on a date,'" Stella mimics in an Australian accent that is damn near perfect.

I scratch the back of my head and sigh, my eyes traveling up and down her figure. I've delighted in it now four times, her buxom ass, the soft and slight curve of her lower belly. It's making me hard just looking at her. "Well, it suits you."

"*Suits* you! I see what you did there," Stella giggles. "Like a swimsuit?"

I blink.

"You didn't mean to do that?"

I shake my head. "Giving me more credit than I deserve for a pun like that."

Stella shrugs. "Think faster next time." Then with the grace of an Olympic swimmer, she dives into the water.

I'm used to women who don't want to get their hair wet and who can't imagine breaking a nail. She's down for almost anything except capitalism, which is a big one in my book, but her free-spiritedness speaks to my soul.

When she comes up above the water, she grins. "Come on in! Water's warm."

Unlike the poolside back in Santorini, there are no prying eyes watching our every move. Here, I have no one to impress. Except for Stella. So, I fling off my shirt and dive in after her, a bit clumsier, but still.

We float around for a bit, enjoying the beautiful sunlight and water softly lapping around us. Then, Stella swims over to the rocky plateau and finds that the water gets shallow enough to stand in. I follow her, gliding through the water until my feet touch the bottom, sooner than hers could. "You're right. The water's nice."

She shrugs. "Of course, I'm right."

I smile, but again, when her hazel eyes meet mine, I look away.

What's wrong with you, man? You've been inside her and you can't make a little eye contact?

Her eyes are Colin's eyes. When I see that brown edged in green, all I think about is how I've betrayed my friend.

"Did you see Adelaide's face when we were boarding the boat?"

I look back at her with a frown. "No. I didn't even know she was watching."

"Of course, she was," Stella says, crossing her arms. "From the aft."

"Well, what was her face?"

Stella rolls her eyes and pouts her lips out, trying to recreate a face I know well. The judgement of Adelaide Frazer. "Like this," she says.

"You look like a fish," I laugh.

"Well, you know what I mean," she says, waving her hands as if it doesn't matter. "She looked pissed. That's all."

"Now, why would she be pissed that I'm going on an excursion with my 'girlfriend'?" I ask in a teasing lilt, pushing myself toward Stella in the water until we're toe to toe, and I can crane my lips down to hers.

Stella looks away before I can do the deed, though. "Because she's not over you."

My eyes widen as if I've been slapped in the face. "She's getting married."

"So? Why would she invite you here if not to keep tabs on you and try and make you jealous? I think she just wanted to get you back under her spell."

"You know I've *been* under her spell. She didn't need to drag me here to do that."

Stella looks away from me. "Just saying."

What I want to tell Stella but can't is that for the first time in the two years since Adelaide left me, the spell isn't working. She's right in front of me and I don't give a shit about her.

I only have eyes, mind, and body for Stella.

I'll have to work that out in therapy in a week.

"Hey," I say softly, tilting her chin up toward mine. "Look at me."

Hazel against blue. I don't look away this time.

"I'm not thinking about her right now, Stella." Feels safe enough because it's true and doesn't betray the depth of my growing feelings for her.

She smiles, and this time, she lets me lean down and kiss her. And kiss her, and kiss her...

In the blink of an eye, I have her pressed up against the rocky sea wall. I'm already hard. God, I've really got it bad for her. "Turn around," I murmur between kisses.

Stella doesn't move fast enough for me, so I spin her around, pressing my cock up against the back of her ass, her hips flush with the rock. She gasps.

"I want you here. Can I have you here?" I ask against her temple, slick curls against my lips.

I feel her nod. "Yes. God, yes."

I reach under the water and pull the crotch of her bikini aside, then unsheathe myself. The good thing about fucking so much in such a short period of time is we are both eagerly primed for one another over and over. I pop inside her, relish the complicated moan she emits and then let the pleasure of her tight pussy hit me. It's like standing up when you've been drinking, not realizing how drunk you really are. A brilliant, strange high.

I start to bob back and forth inside her, the water creating resistance on my hips. Stella's head lolls back on my shoulder in pleasure, her breath landing against my wet neck.

"You make it impossible to resist you," I murmur to her.

"Flynn..." Her hand grips a ridge of rock, and she whimpers. "Baby..."

I can't resist her when she calls me names. Even when they're the sweetest things you've ever heard. I lay my hand on top of hers, giving me the leverage to pump faster into her. "Look at me."

She does, but it lasts only a minute before my forehead falls to hers. I grunt, arousal swelling inside me. I forget about our magical surroundings. If anything, it makes this tryst feel even more secret and contained. Like our own mythology. Just for us.

Stella reaches her free hand around my jaw, kissing me softly, then rakes her fingers back through my hair. "Keep going. I got you."

Am I the only one that seems to be spiraling out of control? We are creating tiny waves with our thrusts. Our moans create echoes off the rocks. It all swirls around us, setting the scene for an absolute explosion between us.

I drop my mouth to her shoulder, tasting seawater and a trace of sunscreen. "Oh god, I have to..."

"You have to, baby, you have to," she says, almost pleading with me.

That's when the dynamite lights. One more thrust and then I break, a violent moan against her shoulder, my body shaking as I try to hold her as close to me as possible, and my cock releases everything I had saved since this morning. Shouldn't be that much, but with Stella... well, she's milking me dry.

"Give me your hand," she whispers raggedly to me.

I catch her meaning without asking for clarification. I slide my hand into the crotch of her suit, my fingers skimming her clit. From the groan she emits, I know I've struck gold: that perfect blossom of her clitoris.

I jerk my hand back and forth over her clitoris. Perhaps if I wasn't still clouded from orgasm, I would take a bit more time and be a bit more careful, but I want to give her the pleasure she's just given me and then some. "I'll make you come, don't worry. I'd never walk away before you've –"

Lucky for me, Stella was not far from her peak. Barely a minute of me working her and she's bending her neck over my shoulder; her chest heaves with a moan, perfect breasts arching toward the sky. I remain strong for her. I've got her. She won't fall.

I'd never let that happen.

Stella melts in my arms, panting.

I kiss her softly on the jaw. "So good. You're so good."

Stella merely smiles. Entirely spent.

I turn around and take her limp arms over her shoulders. "Hold onto me. I'll take you back."

We swim back to the dock and spend the rest of our time in the grotto with our legs intertwined as we devour every last bite of the picnic. Brie, a French baguette, chocolate-covered strawberries, honey wine... all so delicious. In between conversation and laughter, I can't help but glance her way with all the longing in my heart. It's a longing that has existed without me knowing for a long time.

The truth is becoming clear. Now that I have Stella Banks, I'm not sure I'm going to be able to let her go.

Chapter 12

Stella

When Flynn told me the group was touring the Kotor for the day, I mistakenly imagined a historical tour. I had read in my googling about beautiful, unsung churches and fortresses dating back hundreds of years.

Silly me, thinking my cruise companions want anything to do with historical tours. No, very much the opposite.

Today, we're shopping. To hell with the beautiful scenery and all the history. We've opted for a "tour" of the premier Porto Montenegro, which boasts luxury shops that all these gals can easily find walking down Fifth Avenue.

I can't *really* complain. I get to walk around on Flynn's arm the entire day, watching everyone go gaga for Dior purses and Rolex watches.

Flynn is really a man after my own heart. The two of us hang back at every store, merely taking a gander around and then finding the nearest place to sit where we can chat and idly touch each other's hands.

It's gushy, I know. I can't explain it, but for the past three days, I've been over the moon about our "fake" affair.

Although, it's starting to rub people the wrong way. Namely, Adelaide.

"If you two are just going to sit there with bedroom eyes, I think you should go back to the boat," she says, walking past us with her nose in the air.

Flynn and I exchange a look. Neither of us is going to mention that Flynn mentioned that to Adelaide before we left the boat, and *she* explicitly said no. "Sorry, would you rather me save them for someone else?" I ask with a tone naïve enough she just might think I'm an idiot.

She throws her hands up in the air and walks through the racks of clothes to find Theo, glomming onto him immediately and moping into his shoulder.

"Remind me what you saw in her?" I ask Flynn.

"If I'm entirely honest, it's probably not what I saw in her, but on her if you catch my drift."

And do I ever. Adelaide is picture-perfect. No wonder she's a model. Why would he settle for me and my Birkenstocks when he can have nearly six feet of pure goddess?

"I've matured quite a bit since then," Flynn adds.

"Oh, have you?"

"Yes."

I give him a sneaking smile. "Are you saying that you don't think I'm cute?"

"When did I say that?!" Flynn gapes.

"Just that you see what's on the inside rather than what's on the outside," I say, gesturing to my outfit. Khaki shorts and a crop top. Not exactly luxury.

"Now, you're just putting words in my mouth, Stella." He leans toward me, mouth to my ear. "*You* are the full package."

If we're still playing pretend, we don't need to compliment each other or exchange sweet nothings. And he certainly doesn't need to kiss me when no one is looking. And yet here we are. Three days deep into our real affair, nine into our "fake" one.

"Don't worry about her. She's just jealous."

We're interrupted by Cash's droll Aussie accent. She's already hit the stores hard today, with bags hanging off both her arms. "Jealous?" I ask.

"Of course!" Cash sits on the arm of my chair and looks down at me and Flynn. "Don't think we haven't all noticed how the two of you have just come to life the past few days. It's hard to ignore. You're making us *all* jealous."

I flush, glancing at Flynn. "Sorry."

"Are you kidding?! No, no. I'm teasing you. Besides..." Cash looks off in the distance at Adelaide. "She deserves to be humbled."

Yeesh. I hope my friends aren't saying things like that at *my* engagement party.

A bit later, we're heading out of the store, on the hunt for lunch.

"You're sure you don't want anything?" Flynn murmurs as we walk past another store.

"It's not my speed." I pat his arm. "Besides, you're not buying me anything."

"I'd be happy to. Seriously."

There's something in his voice that's almost desperate. This is why the upper echelons of society boggle my mind. They have all the money in the world and know that any big purchase for them is just a drop in the bucket, yet simultaneously understand it to be a prime show of affection.

"What would Colin say if I were carrying around a Gucci purse?" I snort.

"Well, Gucci wouldn't be your speed, but something from Versace would –"

I smack Flynn on the arm. "Don't even think about buying me Versace."

He laughs. He's showing his teeth more. His canines are quite pointy, but unlike all his friends, he doesn't have veneers. Just Flynn. Makes me smile.

"Hey, lovebirds –" Franklin catches up to us and nods up ahead. "You've got a stop to make."

I frown. "What are you talking about?"

Will appears on the other side of Flynn. "We're not letting you be trapped in two years of will-they-won't-they like Wadeltsky and Frazer." Will and Franklin loop their arms through ours and pull us ahead of the group toward the store.

"Guys, seriously, we're just having a nice time, can we –" Flynn tries to argue with them, but they silence him.

"Not taking no for an answer!" Franklin practically sings.

They march us directly into Bulgari, jewels sparkling in every direction it practically blinds me.

"Excuse me!" Will cries out, smacking Flynn on the back. "We're looking for an engagement ring!"

"Could I see the green one?" My mouth is dry as I point down into the jewelry case at a necklace that could probably pay for the downpayment on a new car.

The saleswoman, although it feels wrong to call her that because she looks like a villainous queen in the best way possible with her severe bun and high cheekbones, removes the necklace from the case. "Eighteen karat rose gold set with malachite and pave diamonds. Incredibly elegant. Would suit your eyes, don't you think?" she poses her final question to Flynn.

"Y-yes."

We've been able to move the woman away from showing us engagement rings and are now just indulging her by letting her try and sell us a necklace. At this point, it's only out of politeness since Will and Franklin abandoned us in hopes of finding something to eat. Neither of us can bring ourselves to tell her "no" when we've wasted her time.

"You mind if I put it on her?" Flynn asks.

"Of course, Mr. Madden." The woman gestures toward a mirror behind us.

She knew who he was when she set eyes on him. No doubt she'll keep this story and sell it to the press.

Flynn takes the necklace and eyes me. I step over to the mirror and face it. This is the first time I've really seen Flynn and me together, side by side, since we've started our dalliance. And though our sense of style is very different, I have to say it's a nice picture. I could picture this portrait on my Instagram or a Christmas card or an engagement announcement.

If you don't stop it right now...

"Okay, let's see here..." Flynn brings his arms around my neck, positioning the pendant of the necklace at my clavicle. The chill of gold makes me shiver. "I've always been terrible with these things," he mutters, fumbling with the clasp.

I giggle. "It's alright. You're doing great."

"There." He draws his hands away and looks back into the mirror. A smile crosses his lips as he looks at the fan-shaped necklace against my skin.

"It is very beautiful," the woman helping us calls out from the counter.

"Of course, she'd say that," I say softly so only Flynn can hear.

He laughs, giving her a smile. "Yes, I think so too."

Does he really mean it?

He turns back to me, pursing his lips. "Stella, let me just buy it, and then we can get out of here."

I touch the pendant and rip my hand away as if it's scorched me. "No, Flynn, I'm not letting you do that."

"Please, it's nothing."

"I'd never wear it."

His brow tightens. Have I hurt him? "Then pick out something you would wear. I'd like to buy it for you."

"We've already been over this."

"Stella, how else are you going to remember me?"

The word remember stabs me in the gut. We're already planning our demise when we've just started. That's how it has to be. It's romantic of him, I'll give him that. But a Bulgari pendant made of gold and diamonds will look out of place. "Fine. You can buy me a piece of jewelry."

Flynn's face lights up, eyes crinkling at the sides.

"But not from here."

His face falls again; before he has time to protest, I turn around to the saleswoman. "Can you direct us to the closest flea market around here?"

The Kotor Bazar is built into a section of the Old City wall, nestled in between two beautiful, aged churches. It took a short car ride to get here, but it's so worth it. Though it's mostly tchotchkes and souvenirs, it's much more my speed than stuffy Bulgari.

We look high and low, past lanterns and ornaments, t-shirts and bucket hats, decorative plates and spoons… until finally, we find a red-roofed booth manned by an elderly man working on whittling away a piece of wood.

At his station are rows and rows of carved wooden necklaces. Each one is unique due to its handmade nature.

The man looks at us with a cold look in his eye.

"These are beautiful," I say.

His face softens and he nods. "Thank you," he says, deep voice rumbling.

"So intricate."

"You like these?" Flynn asks, not with judgment but curiosity.

"I think it matches me better than what we saw back there, don't you think?"

Flynn nods, smiling.

"Okay!" I step back and pat him on the arm. "Go ahead!"

"Go ahead what?"

"Pick one out!"

Flynn raises an eyebrow. "You want me to –"

"Yes…"

"But I want you to like it. To wear it. You know, I don't want to –"

I grab his hand and squeeze. "I'll like it if it's from you. Whatever it is. Promise."

He chews on his lower lip. I can tell he's nervous. Adorable how much weight he's putting on this. "Alright." He leans over the display, poring over each and every necklace. I'm not sure how long we're there for, but it's long enough that I'm starting to wonder if people are staring.

Flynn finally points to one. "This one."

I stay back, not wanting to influence his choice, and watch as he hands over several euros to the man. Then, he turns back to me, holding the necklace up in one hand. Dangling there at the end of a leather necklace loop is what looks to be a seabird in flight, polished wings poised for the dive.

"Do you like it?" Flynn asks.

I smile. "Why a bird?"

"Well..." Flynn steps behind me and puts the necklace around my neck. The wood feels much better than the gold. "I guess it's a bit basic to say you're free. But that's what I've come to... respect about you. I didn't understand it until now."

I touch the bird on my chest and then turn around. "I love it. Thank you."

"You haven't even seen it on you."

I shake my head. "Don't have to."

I don't have to see it to know I love it. "Thank you."

Flynn considers my face for a long moment. Like he might say something. Something important.

"You hungry?"

Sigh. Maybe next time.

Chapter 13

Flynn

The days have gone by faster than I would like. Isn't that the tragedy of happiness? Time just flies when things feel good. When waking up isn't a chore, and you aren't slogging through your day from meeting to meeting, life just blows right past you.

Stella makes me feel in the moment. I know it certainly helps that we're in one of the most idyllic locations on earth; the Mediterranean in summer is proof that Mount Olympus must exist. The glimmering blue waters, open sweeping skies, and craggy, ancient rocks are enough proof for me.

And that says a lot considering I'm a businessman. I don't work in imagery and metaphors. I like proven facts and figures.

But again, that must be Stella's doing.

When I am away from her, even if only for a few moments, I find my body and soul yearning to return to her.

I understand why the other guests are starting to get annoyed by us. They don't realize that what's happening between us is a honeymoon phase. That our history began just a few days ago, which is why there's no way we could keep our hands off each other even if our lives depended on it.

Just last night at dinner, Stella's hand kept inching up my thigh under the table. We thought we were being sly until I caught Adelaide's eye across the table, her laser stare boring into my soul.

The funny thing was, I didn't care.

Not about this being her party, not about her being upset with me...

I'm starting not to care about Adelaide at all.

All those feelings I have poured into her over the past two years now all belong to Stella.

I can't tell her this, of course. Otherwise, it might be impossible for us to part when we get back to the States. Best not to complicate things with the subjectivity of feelings when we have a plan that is measured and objective.

Today, as has become our afternoon habit, we are laying out on the bow of the boat. We are "tanning." Although that's really just code for fondling each other under the Croatian sun. Sometimes people join us. Cash and Gregory, or the footballers and their wives.

We behave around them. Sort of, at least.

But when it's just us...

"Are you falling asleep?" Stella murmurs, tucking her head up against my chest.

"Hm? No." I must have been zoning out, thoughts coming like flurrying snow. "How could I sleep when I know I don't have a moment to waste..." I wrap my arm tighter around her and put my lips against a spray of curls on top of her head. "...being with you?"

Stella giggles. Her body relaxes fully into me. Our touch has become easier and easier with each passing day. Like it's something we've both longed for.

"Baby. You're buzzing," Stella says.

I frown. "Is that slang for being hard or something?"

"No, it's –"

"Because I'm always –" I kiss the hinge of her jaw. "*Buzzing* for you then."

"Flynn!" Stella smacks her hand against the pocket of my trunks. "I'm talking about your phone!"

I suddenly notice the vibrating in my pocket. "Oh, you meant like literally buzzing."

She laughs. "But while we're at it, I wouldn't mind having you hard, either."

Stella presses a few kisses to the front of my neck, and I sigh. I want to just let the phone ring, but phone calls can't just go to voicemail when I've been away from the office for nearly two weeks. I fish the phone out of my pocket, trying to ignore how her touch is making me feel.

All my arousal immediately disappears when I see it's Colin who is calling. "Stella –"

"You can answer, I'll keep going," she says in a lusty voice.

"It's your brother."

She stops, drawing away from me. Her hazel eyes are wide, with squiggled lines of fear across her brow. "Oh."

"I should take it." I haven't talked to Colin since we were in Montenegro, and even then, it's only been a few texts back and forth. The guy must be floundering, getting the VR presentation ready to go for our investors.

"Go ahead. I'll be here," she says, the corners of her lips drawing back with shame.

I scramble to my feet and walk to the railing of the boat to answer. "Hello?" My voice cracks. *Wow, Flynn, way to sound suspicious.*

"What the fuck is wrong with you."

My heart pounds in my chest. It's abundantly clear from the way he answers that this call has nothing to do with Wired Reality. It has to do with Stella. "You'd have to talk to my therapist about that one," I say, attempting a lame joke.

"You crossed a fucking line."

He knows. How does he know? Unless Adelaide somehow has a pipeline to Colin to funnel information, I'm not sure how he could possibly be upset or suspicious. "What the hell are you talking about, Colin?"

Innocent until proven guilty, I guess.

"You and Stella. You're – you promised me you wouldn't do anything."

"And I haven't!"

"Then why are your pictures all over the internet?"

I feel the blood drain from my face. Yes, the paparazzi have been following us around. But when we're on excursions, we still have to put up a front so that the people with us don't suspect we've been pretending. Even though we're not pretending anymore. My head is spinning just thinking about how complicated Stella and I have made this. "What pictures?"

"I'm sending them."

I pull the phone away from my ear and wait for a text to come through from Colin. Only a few seconds later, a picture appears in our chat.

It's a grainy photo of Stella and me on the bow of the boat. We're in the same position we were just in before Colin interrupted with his phone call. Stella draped over my chest, a big smile on her face. My hand is in her hair, playing with her curls. She's wearing the sunglasses I purchased for her before the trip. She's been playing with the wardrobe I promised to provide for her, always adding her funky accessories to go along with it.

Around her neck, I can see the outline of her bird necklace. She hasn't taken it off since I gave it to her.

"Flynn!" I hear Colin shout through the phone. It's not on speakerphone, but it might as well be, given the volume of his voice.

"Y-yeah!" I shout in reply.

"What the fuck is –"

"Colin, the point was –" I glance back at Stella. She's been joined by Cash, Gregory, and Brandy, but their eyes are all focused on me. I clear my throat and lower my voice. "You know what the point of this was."

"Yes, and you promised you wouldn't –"

"We *have to pretend*," I say. "All the time. You have no idea how exhausting it is. That's just acting."

Colin is quiet. "It doesn't look like acting."

I swallow. I should have prepared him better for this. "I promise, Colin. We always have eyes on us. And Adelaide is always sniffing around. She knows me so well she can see right through me."

As soon as I say that I realize how untrue it is. Adelaide has never known me well. I'm not sure if that was her fault or mine. We chased after the idea of each other, me the baby genius billionaire, her the international supermodel. Did we ever really meet in the middle? Did we ever really know each other?

"Dammit, Flynn, I want to believe you but –"

"Trust me. Nothing is going on between me and Stella." I break my own heart saying that. "I promise. You can ask her too."

Colin hesitates, but finally sighs. Yielding. "No. I believe you. I just – I knew you had to pretend, but actually seeing it is –"

"Trust me, Stella still hates my guts. When we got to sleep at night, she puts a line of pillows between us on the bed."

Colin chuckles. "Okay. That's good. As long as you're still enemies."

"Yeah... totally."

"Anyway. Sorry I interrupted you, I –"

"I get it. You had to. I can't blame you. If it was my sister, I'd do the same."

"Thanks for understanding, Flynn."

A lump of shame manifests in my throat.

"How are things at the office?" I ask.

"You don't want to hear about that. Just enjoy your last few days before you get back to the grind, okay?"

I can't respond before Colin hangs up the phone, retreating sheepishly from his accusation. I hate gaslighting people. But I must protect him from the truth. Besides, it won't be true in a couple of days. It will have been a blip. An anomaly.

"Everything okay?" Stella calls out.

I turn back around and smile at the sight of Stella cradling Brandy's head in her lap, making a small braid in the side of her hair.

"Sounded intense, Madden," Cash adds, picking at her nails.

"Oh, it was nothing. He's just freaking out over our presentation and –"

"I should call him and talk him down," Stella says.

"No!" I reply, all too intensely. "I mean... it's not that serious. I talked him down."

My eyes land on Stella's. How can her eyes feel so safe and dangerous at the same time? Simultaneously the thing I crave and also a warning that what I want, I can never fully have.

Stella inclines her head to my towel. "Sit, baby."

I sit down and join the group, their conversation idle and trivial. My head is swimming. I can't concentrate.

But then Stella leans over and kisses my temple tenderly. An all-important reminder: I have to enjoy this time with her. Before it's too late.

And I can never have her again.

Chapter 14

Stella

"More shots! Pronto, per favore!" Adelaide yells, a limp Italian accent tainting her words.

I grimace at Flynn. I know if I have anything more to drink, I'm going to be sick as a dog tomorrow morning. Especially since we will be traveling through the day tomorrow to get to Venice for the final evening of the trip.

Flynn touches my back sympathetically. "You want to go to bed?"

I don't want to take him away from the party because, surprisingly, he's having a pretty nice time with his new buddies. They're an unlikely group, but they enjoy themselves immensely when they're together. Flynn is anything but a bro and sticks out like a sore thumb with his black-rimmed glasses, and yet it somehow works entirely. "No, I think I just need some fresh –"

"Dance!" Cash shouts, grabbing me by the hand and yanking me into a tripping dance to the loud pop music playing through the speakers.

"Cash!" I shout, laughing. She always has a way of pulling me onto the dance floor. If nothing else comes out of this trip, my friendship with Cash will have been worth this whole mess.

"You're just standing there with your boyfriend talking about the next time you're going to fuck! We get it! You *love each other!*"

Though I'm bouncing to the music, my mind is anywhere but here. Love. Do I love Flynn? Surely no more than friends love one another, right?

Right??

I look back at Flynn. He's already shooting the shit with Simon. His cheeks are pinched red from liquor, and his mouth is caught in permanent laughter.

I don't know if he's changed over the past thirteen days or if a part of him he's kept under wraps has just been released. But I adore this side of him. I thought I'd be tending to his unending infatuation with Adelaide, talking him down from that ledge of desperation.

Instead, I've... seen a new, beautiful side of him. A side I very well might love.

After spinning in circles, I'm hit with a wave of nausea. Too much tequila. Luckily, Cash doesn't seem to notice I've let go of her hand and is playfully grinding up against Gregory, who is yelling, "Nope! Don't feel anything!"

Everyone's distracted. If I slip away, no one will notice right away.

I just need five minutes to myself. To clear my head and settle my stomach.

I hurry away and clamor up the stern deck, the highest deck of the ship. When I emerge from the stairs, the expanse of the sky opens up above me. Generous amounts of stars make up constellations, and the moon looks swollen and nearly full.

I take a deep breath and sink down onto the cushions of the bunny pad. The air is suddenly fresh and salty again, not tainted with the scents of luxury perfumes and the sick tinge of alcohol. I tune my ears to the sound of the ocean; the thumping music starts to feel much further away than just the deck below me.

I miss home. Miss my dogs. And I feel guilty for missing home. Because home means I'm leaving Flynn behind.

Don't get me wrong. The Med is beautiful. And the fact I've had the trip of a lifetime for free under the most luxurious circumstances possible isn't lost on me. However, there's no place like home really, is there?

"I've never understood why they call it a poop deck."

I turn and find Flynn at the top of the stairs, leaning on the railing with a smirk on his lips. His linen shirt is unbuttoned just enough to make me shiver at the anticipation of ripping it off him, and he has a cocktail in one hand, muddled with melting ice. "I don't think they call it a poop deck on luxury yachts," I say wryly.

"You think they only save that for naval warships and fishing vessels?" he says, wandering further onto the deck.

I lean back and stretch my body out long. I'm wearing a dress Flynn picked out for me. White and blue stripes. *Very* Martha's Vineyard. The expectations of changing outfits so many times every day have left me with an empty suitcase, and honestly, I don't mind indulging him now. "You really want to come up here and start talking to me about a *poop* deck?"

"Oh, I'm sorry, am I ruining the moment or something?" Flynn asks, pulling one knee up on the bunny pad.

"Kind of! Me, the stars, the moon."

"A threesome."

"Precisely."

Flynn downs the rest of his drink and puts it down on the deck before crawling up onto the bunny pad. "Is there room for one more?"

"Maybe," I say, eyeing him carefully.

Flynn sidles in between my legs, lingering over me. "What if I say please?" he asks and then kisses my collarbone.

"Flynn..." I say with a sigh. There's so much more I want to say. All that I can manifest is his name.

"I get it, I get it. Not trying to force anything," he says, rolling onto his side next to me. I can feel his blue eyes staring at my face, waiting for me to look at him. "What's wrong, Stella?"

My body tightens at the sound of him saying my name.

Flynn hesitantly wraps his arm around my middle. Out of the corner of my eye, I see him frown. "Did I do something?"

I feel tears well up in my eyes. "No, you didn't."

"You're crying."

Not yet. Tears haven't started to fall. But I'm nearly there. And he's noticed.

"What's wrong?"

I shake my head and blink to set my tears free. "Just hold me. Please, just hold me."

Flynn engulfs me in his embrace, his height making me feel so small and safe in his arms. "What's wrong, Stella? Please tell me."

I bury my face in his chest and sob.

He splays a hand out against my back.

"I don't want to go. I don't want..." I lift my head. God, I probably look like a wreck, all snotty and tear-stained. "I don't want to lose you."

Flynn pinches my chin between his fingers. I'm expecting him to tell me that this is the way it must be. It's what we agreed upon. There's no world in which Stella-and-Flynn exist outside of the Mediterranean. "I don't want to lose you either."

I stare at him. "What?"

He brushes a few tears from my cheeks. "I don't want this to end, Stella."

My mouth falls open. I wait for him to add, "But we can't," or something that would inevitably break my heart. But he doesn't. In fact, I can tell he's at a loss for words himself. Didn't expect to say that out loud.

What else can I do but reward him with a kiss?

I wrap myself around him, cocooning him with my ardor as I kiss him fervently.

I've learned him so well that past week. Learned the edges of his ribs and the curve of his spine. I've tried to memorize it carefully so that I never forget. But maybe I won't have to.

Maybe this won't end.

There would be obstacles. But fuck them.

I'm falling in love with Flynn Madden on a yacht in the Mediterranean, and nothing can stop me.

"Stella..." Flynn moans between kisses.

I won't be stopped. "I want you."

"God, I want you."

I grab the waistband of his loose linen pants. "You're buzzing," I tease, rubbing my groin against his, feeling the outline of his perfect cock.

"You could say tha – ahhh..." he trails off as soon as he feels my hand palming him.

"I want you in my mouth." I push the waistband of his pants down, releasing him fully.

"Someone might find us."

"Who cares?"

Flynn chokes on his laugh as I wrap my lips around his cock.

I've had it in my mouth before. Salty against my tongue. The delectable smell that I can only describe as pheromones. I lap him up deeper and deeper, watching his face intently for his reactions.

He is wracked with pleasure, mouth hung open, eyes despondent as he knows he's entirely at my mercy.

Makes me so fucking wet.

I take him all the way in, letting the head of his cock hit the back of my throat. I gag and draw my mouth away, but before I can return, Flynn shakes his head. "On top of me. Please."

"How can I say no to that?"

I straddle him quickly, his saliva-coated cock right between my thighs.

"Let me see you…" Flynn moans, running his hand down the buttons of my dress.

I pulse my hips against him while I undo the buttons of my dress, each one exposing my naked body to the salty ocean air. I watch how his face lights up, his drunken, lazy eyes devouring my beauty.

I don't know if I would have described myself that way before this trip. I'm not the type of woman who believes a man can change me or that his word means it's true. But I can't deny how powerful it feels to see the way Flynn reacts to me. Like I'm something divine.

A goddess.

Flynn places his hands against my hips and lets his hands travel up my body slowly, feeling every inch of my torso until he reaches my breasts and cups them softly. "The night… it looks good on you. You're glowing."

I can't hold back a smile.

Flynn guides my hips over his, pressing the head of his cock against my pussy. I sink my hips down, watching how my body consumes him. "Meant for you, I'm... meant for you." Pleasure makes my words cryptic. I mean my body, but maybe I mean more than that.

"Yes, you are, baby," he murmurs, tucking his hands under my dress and against my bare back. "I fit inside you perfectly."

I start to bob my hips up and down onto him, letting out a long sigh. God, he feels so good. My head dips back as a helix of pleasure forms through me. The heavens up above me, the mythology of constellations, and the sadness of the moon. We are the next story to add to the canon, Flynn and me. I feel like our bodies will burst into thousands of stars and create an image that people millennia from now will look at to remember our story.

Flynn latches his hands around my hips and pushes himself off the cushion, driving himself deep inside me. "Can't help it. Can't wait," he mutters.

Suddenly, I'm not in control. He's thrusting up into me at a breakneck speed, reaching the deepest part of me he can. The helix tightens inside me, sparking, setting parts of me alight. "Don't stop, *please*, don't stop!"

Flynn shakes his head and bites his bottom lip.

I emit a low moan that bounces along with his rhythm. It gets louder and louder. I forget there are people on the deck just below us who might hear us over the music. But fuck them. I don't care. I'm getting what's mine.

And Flynn... Flynn is mine.

"Oh, I'm –" I gasp, the feeling so powerful I almost try to pull myself off him. "It's happening, I'm –"

My entire body jolts to life as an orgasm rips through me. I keen at the feeling, so hot and luscious I feel like I might be incinerated right here.

Flynn seizes under me, his hips slamming against mine as if he could be any deeper. Wide blue eyes find mine, full of lust. He grabs me by the shoulders and pulls me down so our chests are pressed together.

"*Fuck*," he curses in my ear before letting out a loud grunt and releasing inside me.

For nearly a minute afterward, all I can hear is my blood rushing in my ears mixed with our panting. We've had sex so many times since we started, and somehow, it only gets better.

If I were to rank them, this time was most certainly the best.

Now that we're done hiding how we feel, I think we might be unstoppable.

Flynn hugs me tight and pushes his face into the crook of my shoulder. He doesn't say anything. But I can feel it.

Don't let me go. Don't leave. I want you. Forever.

Chapter 15

Flynn

Tonight, Stella and I were forbidden from sitting next to one another. Apparently, people are officially fed up with us.

Stella is sitting on the opposite side of the table from me, a few seats down, looking as elegant as a Roman goddess. As this is the last dinner of the trip, Adelaide arranged for all the girls to get done up. I thought Stella might try to refuse, but she went along with it. For my sake, I think.

The stylist has put her hair up into a brilliant updo, leaving two curls out to frame her face. And her face, which has so rarely been touched by a makeup brush, is contoured and highlighted. Her lips painted with dark burgundy lipstick.

If looks could kill, well, Stella Banks would get the electric chair.

Throughout dinner, all we've been able to do is exchange longing glances. Nothing more. I can't wait to get my hands on her later, though.

We've decided to leave talking about what's going on between us for the plane ride tomorrow. I'm having her join me on my private jet rather than flying commercial. There'll be plenty of time and space for us to really get a grip on reality.

It will be hard to bring our relationship into the real world. Maybe we'll go on a few dates and remember our original disdain for one another. Maybe Colin will completely freak out and make everything too difficult.

Regardless, we both want to try. We both want to *risk*.

"You're awfully quiet, Flynn."

Unfortunately, I've been seated right next to Adelaide. I didn't have a choice, at least according to the place cards.

Adelaide is leaning towards me with her elbow on the arm of the chair. "Am I?" I ask, with a touch of exasperation in my voice.

"Well..." she eyes Stella briefly. "You're not talking to me."

"What would you like to talk about, Adelaide?" I ask, raising my eyebrows expectantly.

She pouts. "You say that like you don't want to talk to me."

I start to reply, but she's not done.

"In fact, we've barely talked this whole trip."

"Well –"

"You've been so preoccupied with your new girlfriend you've barely spent any time with me."

I blink. "Adelaide, we haven't spoken in two years."

She touches my arm. "Then we have a lot of catching up to do."

I glance at Theo beside her. He's caught up in conversation with his bros. Not paying a speck of attention to what his new fiancé might be doing. I always wondered what she saw in him, but now that I've met him, I wonder what he sees in her, other than her obvious exterior beauty. He's goofy and friendly, and doesn't take things too seriously. Adelaide always has a bee in her bonnet. It definitely seems to be a case of opposites attract.

Makes me wonder what I ever saw in her.

"I thought you'd be excited to see me," Adelaide says softly. For once, she sounds like a human.

I clear my throat. "I was. I am."

"Don't lie."

We exchange a look. Her usual posturing has been dropped; I can see the girl that I knew. Far away, but still, she's there. Her pretty green eyes needing reassurance, and her hand desperately needing to be held.

No, Flynn. It's not real. I have the real thing. She's only a few seats away. I won't be tempted by the empty joy of Adelaide Frazer.

"You know why I brought you here, don't you? Don't you get it yet?"

I furrow my brow in bewilderment. "Huh?"

Adelaide sighs, eyes rolling toward her fiancé and then back to me. "Don't you see how ridiculous this is?" she whispers. "Me and him?"

She's bold to speak about this while he's sitting right next to her. And what the fuck is going on right now?

"Besides, he's not even that good of a football player."

I shake my head. Nothing is making sense. This isn't adding up. "You left me for him, Adelaide."

"I know I did," she says carefully.

"And you didn't speak to me for two years."

"Because you never tried, Flynn. I was waiting for you to be a man and –"

No. I will not allow her to sit here and tell me what *I* should have done to fix my broken heart. I will not be told I had an opportunity to have her back if only I'd grown a pair. Because I had thought about it. Time after time. Colin told me not to. Hell, Stella told me not to a couple of times when I needed a little extra reassurance, and she was able to put our rivalry aside.

But now that Adelaide is telling me things might have been different if I had fought for her... begged, maybe.

My head is spinning.

"Flynn, baby –" Adelaide grabs my wrist.

I yank it away and stand up in a rush. My chair scrapes the floor loudly, garnering the attention of everyone at the table. I can feel Stella's eyes on me. She's obviously worried.

I don't deserve her.

"I... um..." *Deep breath.* "Bathroom," I say, and then skitter away from the group.

I don't know where the fuck I'm going as I weave in and out of servers and guests of the flouncy Venetian restaurant. I'm sure I hear my name called out a few times, "Mr. Madden, may I help you?"

But no one can help me. Not right now.

I finally make it to the front door and burst forth into the hot summer night. The street is still dense with people; there's a line to get into the restaurant to my left, and a palazzo filled with activity to the right. Fucking Italy. Just like New York. You can never be alone.

"Flynn!" I hear Adelaide's voice call after me.

I start to quickly walk down the street toward one of the canals. I will happily get lost in the throes of Venice for a few hours, allowing the scent of dying fish to clear my head.

From behind me, I hear Adelaide's high heels clicking after me. Damn, how the hell can she run in those? "Flynn, please wait! I'm getting blisters."

I'm halfway over a bridge when she finally gets to me, her hand glomming onto my arm, nails digging through my sleeve. "Stop, please just –"

"What do you want?" I spit, turning around angrily on my heels to face her.

Her blonde hair has fallen out of place, but, of course, her makeup is still pristine even after practically sprinting after me.

"This is all so fucked, isn't it?" Adelaide asks. She touches my arms softly, gazing up at me.

"You shouldn't have invited me."

"Then why did you come? To show off your little girlfriend with her Birkenstocks and Boho clothes?"

I clench my fists at my sides. "Don't talk about her like that."

"Flynn, what we had was real. I never stopped thinking about you. I only wanted to know you were thinking about me and then –"

"You actually would have come back?" I ask in disbelief.

Adelaide hesitates. "Maybe."

Maybe. Typical Adelaide. She is the type of woman doomed to want what she doesn't have. She will never be happy. That's what fame and fortune do to you. Always makes you seek out the next shiny thing.

"People aren't *things*, Adelaide. You can't just discard them and buy a new one."

"I know that, Flynn, I know that..." She slides her hands up from my arms to my face, as I desperately attempt to move away from her as quickly as possible. "Let me make it up to you. Let me try again."

I start to shake my head.

"I'll break things off with Theo. Tonight. We'll get on a plane. We'll fly somewhere far away. Just you and me, away from all this mess. And we'll pick up where we left off. Can we do that?"

My cheek flinches as fury burns inside me. She is so fucking entitled. How could she possibly think I'd agree to this?

"Please, Flynn."

I don't even have time to react when Adelaide tugs on my head and pushes her lips up against mine. I turn my head as quickly as possible to avoid her lips, but it's too late.

Suddenly, the flash of a camera goes off, followed by a flurry of several more. I get a burst of fortitude and push Adelaide off me, scanning the crowd of paparazzi that have found us here on the bridge.

Adelaide clings to me again, her hand on my chest. "Oh my god, how did they get here?"

It's the tone of her voice, the hollow disingenuousness that catches me off-guard. She's never been a good actress. And her feigned surprise is proof of that.

She planned this somehow. She wanted us to get caught. A way to get into the news cycle, a PR stunt, I don't know what it is, and I don't care. I'm done.

I push Adelaide off me again and elbow my way through the blockade of paparazzi on the bridge. I've got to get out of here.

However, at the end of the bridge stands Stella.

From the look in her eyes, I know she saw everything.

"Stella –" I say, going toward her. "Let me explain."

But I'm not fast enough. She backs away and then breaks off into a sprint in the other direction. I try to run after her, but she's quicker. I lose her as she weaves through the crowd.

It's too late. She saw the kiss. How am I going to convince her that I want nothing to do with Adelaide and that it was all a PR stunt?

I now know the only thing worse than falling in love with my best friend's sister is breaking her heart.

Chapter 16

Stella

First class is no fun when you're depressed. It doesn't matter how many complimentary drinks they offer you or how much legroom you have. None of it makes up for a hole in your heart.

The image of Adelaide and Flynn is scored on my brain. I close my eyes and I can see it, the two of them locked in an embrace, lips pressed in a needy kiss.

In hindsight, I guess it's my fault I saw it. I went after both of them after Flynn made his sudden exit, followed by Adelaide. I knew something was up. I just thought it had more to do with her egging him on or being cruel.

Not... whatever this was.

I watched Adelaide get closer and closer until I was elbowed out of the way by the paparazzi so they could get their shot for their magazines.

They weren't fast enough, though. I saw the moment their lips connected as clear as day, not blinded by the camera flash.

I've had to remind myself dozens of times since just last night that Adelaide was the purpose of my being here. Whatever came up between Flynn and me was a mistake. It was always about her.

Beside me, a woman is reading a British gossip magazine with the image of Flynn and Adelaide on the front. I try not to look at it, but it's impossible. *Reunited and it feels so MESSY* reads the cover. *You can say that again...*

The moment Flynn saw me, I could tell he had regret. But was it regret for kissing her or regret for being caught? I wasn't going to stick around and hear his excuses. It would just remind me of all the things I've never been able to stand about him. The entitlement. The pretension. The lack of concern about anyone but himself.

That wasn't the Flynn I fell in love with though, was it? Was that man even real?

I bury my face in my palm and blink. Tears slide down my cheeks for the billionth time since last night. God, it's embarrassing. I'm so tired of crying over a man who has only ever cared about what I could do for him.

Not about who I am.

"Oh, dear, are you crying?" the woman beside me asks.

"No, no, I'm fine. I'm –"

"Pish!" She drops the magazine on the armrest between us and starts to shuffle around in her purse. "Don't need to pretend around me, dearie. All is fair in love and plane travel. Let me get you a tissue."

As she rustles around in her bag, I can't help but stare at the magazine. It's opened to a picture of Flynn and me on the bow of the boat. I'm lying on my side, back to the camera. I wince at how my bikini bottom is half stuck in my ass. Flynn is facing me, adjusting a lock of my hair, face clear to the camera. The caption of the picture reads, "Taken isn't a word in Flynn Madden's vocabulary."

My eyes well with more tears, and I start to sob.

"Oh, hold on, I've almost got them. Don't you worry your pretty head." The woman finally finds a smushed packet of Kleenex and hands them to me. "Here, all for you."

"Th-thank y-y-you," I warble, ripping the package open and blowing my nose.

"There, there, dear. You want to tell me about it?"

I shake my head. "Nothing to tell."

The older woman sighs heavily. "I've been there. Been there indeed. Well, that's alright. You just cry it out."

She rubs my back softly as I weep. It's very comforting.

Until she starts to chuckle to herself and nods toward the magazine. "Take a little comfort that whatever you're dealing with isn't what we read about in the tabloids, eh?"

And just like that, the floodgates open right up again.

Colin picks me up from JFK and the moment I get in the car, he has a million and one questions.

"Are they together now?"

"I don't know."

"Did you see it coming?"

"No."

"How do you feel?"

"Fine."

He can obviously tell something is wrong; after all, he's my big brother. But he's deciding not to pry. For now.

"Well, I'm already doing damage control," Colin grumbles.

"Sorry to hear that."

"You know, our investors hate when shit like this happens. This is the equivalent of Elon tweeting something stupid. Except worse," Colin explains as he navigates the car through the chaos of arrivals.

I laugh sadly. "Well, then maybe you should have done a better job of convincing him not to go."

I feel Colin's eyes jump to me, but I keep my gaze firmly out the window. "Yeah... maybe," he says and then pauses. "Stella –"

"I'm fine."

"You don't seem fine."

I sigh. "I'm tired." Not just from traveling. From everything. From all of it. *Life*.

"Yes, but it seems like you're... not saying something."

I seal my lips together. "I was stuck on a boat with some of the most horrible people I've ever met, Colin. Not a friend in sight. I'm exhausted."

"I know you and Flynn don't like each other, but you can't say he isn't a friend."

I can say that and more. I can now say he is my *nemesis*. The only thing better than that would be for me not to care a lick about him anymore. I know that's not possible. Not yet. But if I keep away, maybe get over him by getting under someone else, try and convince myself the feelings I was having were just the intoxication of the Mediterranean and all the alcohol, maybe then I'll forget about him.

For now, though, I hate him.

I hate how he made me feel about him.

I hate that even though I hate him I still...I still love him.

"Did he do something, Stella?"

"No!" I answer, a bit too defensively. "I mean... no. He didn't do anything wrong. It was just a mistake for me to go. It was..." I feel my eyes well with tears again. "I'm so tired."

"Hey, hey, hey... it's okay." Colin knows me well enough to know when I'm lying to him. And he also knows when to leave well enough alone. He knows better than to harp on it any longer. "The dogs are going to be so happy to see you."

I feel my insides relax. The thought of my little babies makes the clouds part in the sky, and a smile spread across my face. "Were they good?"

"Yes, although I think I might have been overfeeding them."

"Colin!"

"What?! They're so cute, I can't help it. I'd be a monster not to give them a treat."

We both laugh and then exchange a look. Though he smiles, his brow is still furrowed in concern. I can't look at him for too long without remembering the heartbreak.

"They missed you, Stell."

I nod. "I missed them too."

"And, shockingly, I missed you too."

I smile and lean my head over gently onto Colin's shoulder. He rests his cheek on the top of my head, eyes still glued to the road.

"You can tell me, you know. I won't be mad," he whispers.

Where would I even begin? Even if we hadn't broken the main covenant of this trip, how would I even begin to explain how my thoughts and feelings transformed over the course of two weeks only to leave me desperate and heartbroken, unsure of how to pick up the pieces?

"When you're ready, you can tell me."

I don't reply. Because the truth is I don't think I'll ever be ready to relive those memories. I want to forget the Mediterranean and Flynn Madden as quickly as possible.

Chapter 17

Flynn

I stare out the window of my car at the entrance to Wired Reality. On a normal day, I would do the normal person thing and just get out of my car and go inside.

Except there hasn't been a normal day in two weeks.

Two weeks. Two whole weeks of this shit. I'm about to snap.

Every day since I returned from Venice, the entrance to Wired Reality's corporate office has been swarmed with reporters and photographers. Don't they have anything better to cover right now? Aren't people dying all around the world? Isn't that the *real* news?

Not a CEO playboy kissing a supermodel.

"You want me to go around the block again, Mr. Madden?" my driver asks in a kindly voice.

I look at Freckles beside me. She's been very clingy since I've returned, and honestly, keeping her by my side most hours of the day is good for both of us. She pushes her snout forward; I take it in my hand and give it a soft scratch. Then, I sigh. "No. I don't think they're going anywhere."

The veil of reporters and photographers is thicker than it's been the last few days because Adelaide shot off her mouth. Again. It's not bad enough that she is now in a very public breakup with Theo, now I have to be implicated in it at every turn.

Last night, a clip of Theo on TMZ dropped; the interview asked him if he thought it was karma that his relationship was ending like this. He spouted off a string of expletives so long the cameraman legitimately backed away from him. Then, just this morning, People dropped an issue with Adelaide on the cover with the headline, *"We never stopped loving each other."*

Mind you, I haven't spoken to her since the night she kissed me. I made it very clear once I got back to the boat and saw Stella's things were gone that I would not be speaking to her again.

Maybe Theo deserved the karma for being the other man. But I think I deserve the karma for being hung up on her for so long. I finally got what I thought I wanted… and ruined my whole life in the process.

"Good luck, sir."

I chuckle, grabbing my briefcase and Freckles leash tight in my hand. "Thanks."

I finally get to my office fifteen minutes later with Freckles in my arms like she's a baby. The poor thing was about to get trampled by a reporter from channel seven. She's been shaking since we got in the elevator. To top it off, the left pocket of my suit jacket has been torn asunder, fabric ripped and drooping.

"They're fucking feral out there," I mutter to Colin, who already has set up the latest demo for our medical software.

Colin is silent, tinkering with something on his computer.

I coax Freckles down into her bed I have beside my desk and then shrug off my jacket. "I ought to send them a bill for damages." I toss it to the side. Better a chew toy for the dog than a jacket for me.

Colin still doesn't say anything.

I sigh. Things have been off ever since my return, and we've only talked business. Our presentation for investors is just a week away. I've been busy doing damage control while Colin perfects the program. He's withheld questions just as I've withheld stories. I can sense he suspects something; what I'm not sure.

I've tried to get in touch with Stella many times. All I received was radio silence in return. For a moment, I thought about following what Adelaide said: be a man and don't take no for an answer.

But that's not me. I'm not going to force someone to look at me when it's clear they don't want to.

Especially when it feels like the whole world is looking at me anyway.

Freckles gets up and trots over to Colin. He finally reacts to something other than his computer screen and smiles down at the collie. "Hey, girl."

Freckles jumps on her hind legs and presses her paws into Colin's leg. She's not exactly well trained, but she's a gentle dog and no one seems to mind.

"How are things looking?" I ask while I've got him caught off guard.

Colin's gaze shoots at me, and his mouth tightens into a thin line before he goes back to typing.

I hold up my hands in surrender. "Can I help you with something, or are you just going to give me the silent treatment from now on?"

"I haven't heard from Stella in three weeks."

The sound of her name ties my throat into a knot. I have heard it so seldom in the past three weeks, only in the news when people start to speculate on my relationship status. The last time was a few days ago on Entertainment Tonight when the host announced, "Cheaters!" with an unsettling grin. "Are Adelaide Frazer and Flynn Madden meant for each other? We have the inside scoop."

Whatever scoop they had was not *inside*. But it did include a picture of me and Stella on the boat together, her face hidden by a thrall of curls.

Just that passing image made me miss her all over again. It happens to me several times a day. I'm trying to make it through working hours, trying not to be distracted, and then I'm hit with the memory of her perfume or the sound of her laugh.

I miss her so badly.

"You think something is wrong?" I ask carefully.

"Not in a life-or-death way," Colin says. He finally raises his eyes from the computer and crosses his arms over his chest. "Come on, Flynn. Tell me what happened."

I raise my eyebrows in alarm. "What do you mean?"

"Something happened between you two. I know it. Because she was acting like a weirdo when I picked her up from the airport, and *you* act like a weirdo every second of the day and –"

"I'm fucking stressed! I'm trying to do damage control so our investors –'

"Bullshit. You're avoiding me."

That's... true. It'd be foolish of me to believe he didn't notice. "We're both working hard."

"Stop, Flynn. Just stop," Colin snaps. His hazel eyes... Stella's eyes... fall onto mine. "I want the truth. What did you do to her?"

He asks it like I must have hurt her.

"Did you reject her? Did you make a pass at her?"

"No, no, it was nothing like that."

"Then what?! What was it?"

"We *liked each other!*"

Colin's brow screws together.

"We... what I mean is..." I clear my throat. "The pretending turned into not pretending."

My friend starts to recoil, his face bending with disgust.

"I know... I know we weren't supposed to! I promise we both tried –"

"Oh my God, I knew it. I knew it the second I saw those photos. Neither of you is that good at pretending." He folds his hands over his face. "And then you lied to me about it!"

I bite my lower lip. "I'm sorry."

"I asked you and you lied to me!"

"I know, I just didn't know what to –"

"You could have told me the truth."

"How?! When you made it explicitly clear that we weren't supposed to do more than just tolerate each other?"

Colin winces again. How old is he? Five?? "So let me get this straight. You and Stella started..."

"We were talking about dating when we got back to the States."

"And then you kissed Adelaide?" Without a breath, he jumps across the room toward me and grabs the collar of my shirt. "You cheated on my sister?"

I struggle against Colin's grip. Damn, all that CrossFit is really doing the trick. "Adelaide kissed me! I promise!"

"Likely story!"

"You're hurting me!"

"You broke my sister's heart!"

"Colin, I love her!"

Colin's eyes widen and his hands go slack. I break away and try and catch my breath. "You what?" he asks in a small voice.

"I..." Did I really just say that out loud? "I think I love her."

"You love her or you *think* you love her?"

I feel a migraine coming on. "Colin, don't make me say it again."

Colin blinks. I think for a second he's about to punch me, but instead, he opens his arms wide and embraces me, patting my back. Freckles wants in on the action too, dancing around our feet, pawing our legs.

I'm stunned. "You're... hugging me."

"Of course, I'm hugging you."

"But I did the thing I wasn't supposed to do."

Colin pulls back and nods. "Yeah. You did."

This doesn't make any sense.

"Do you want her back?"

"Huh?"

"These aren't hard questions, Madden! Stop thinking and just act. *Do you want her back?!*"

I stutter briefly, though my chin is nodding before the words come out. "Y-yes."

"Are you willing to fight for her?"

"Yes."

Colin smiles. "Then you've got to get her back."

"But what about what you said about –"

"I'm still pissed, don't get me wrong. But if you love her and are willing to do right by her, I'm not going to stop my sister from getting the type of man she deserves."

I give him a dopey grin. "Are you serious?"

"Yes! Now! To New Jersey! Now!"

My smile fades. "What?!"

"No time like the present!"

I shake my head. "No, I couldn't possibly, I –"

"You want her or not?"

"What if she says no?!"

Colin and I stare at one another. That was a possibility once before when I needed her help pretending to be my girlfriend. Colin was clear then: if Stella says no, it means no. And he doesn't have to say it again. "You at least have to give it a fair shot. One more fair shot, right?" Colin says with a shrug.

"Alright. I'll do it."

"Good man."

I step away and start to reach for my suit jacket until I remember how it was torn to shreds by a reporter. "Best to leave that behind," I say and then check my pockets for my wallet and phone. "Okay, I'm going."

"You're going."

"I'm going."

"Your feet aren't moving."

I look down at my feet, firmly planted in the carpet. "Yeah, I can't move them."

Colin gives Freckles a look. "Come on, girl. You're a herding dog, aren't you?"

The two of them nip at my heels until I'm out the door, and they don't give me a chance to protest before the door is slammed in my face.

Only one thing to do now.

Chapter 18

Stella

"I thought you were joking about that," I say into the phone, leaning my elbows on the reception desk.

Cash laughs through the receiver, bubbly Aussie laugh. "No, I never kid about that."

"Well," I reply with a grimace. "It's not possible. I can't take another day away from the shelter." Especially not now that Flynn's donation has come through. I need to dedicate all my time to planning how we are going to do construction on the yard and still have a place where all these dogs can run around. It's a great way to stay distracted from... literally everything else.

"You don't even know my idea yet! The whole show is going to be in honor of your shelter."

I freeze. "What?!"

She laughs. "I knew that'd get you interested. Listen, it's going to be a very lowkey catwalk, all elevating a good cause."

"Wh-why? I mean, thank you, but –"

"Oh, honey, it's the least I can do after how everything... shook out."

I gulp. "Yeah."

"It was my last straw with Adelaide, really. She used to be such a giving muse. Now she just likes to muck everything up. I don't like that energy. I'm too old for it. Your energy, though, I like. The only requirement I have for the show is you walk in it."

I squeeze my eyes tightly together. Having to strut down a runway showing off my body in fancy clothes sounds like literal hell on earth. But if it can help the shelter... "Alright. I'm in."

"Eeeee! Yes, thank you, darling. Gregory will be in touch with details and –"

The rest of what Cash says is lost on me when Flynn Fucking Madden walks through the front door. My eyes grow wide and my mouth drops.

Flynn takes a few steps toward me and then stops, realizing I'm on the phone.

"Stella? Stella, are you there?" I hear Cash yell through the phone.

"Yes, I'm – yep! All sounds great. Okay, gotta go, goodbye!" I chatter off, not bothering to listen to what she has to say in return. I'm too shocked to care. I drop my phone on the table and go back to staring at Flynn.

"Bad time?" he asks, a nervous but charming smile appearing on his lips.

Any time would be a bad time. "What are you doing here?" I ask coldly.

Flynn half-laughs as if I've just slapped him in the face. "Good to see you too."

I stare at him. "Do you think you deserve something other than disdain after humiliating me in front of the whole world?"

Flynn is dumbfounded. Probably didn't expect me to come out with guns blazing. That was his first mistake.

"Anyway..." I say casually and then go back into the office. I have a list of tasks to get done that has both slipped my mind and been lost on a post-it note.

"Stella, I'd like to talk to you," Flynn calls out.

I hear him walk through the office door behind me. My heart throbs just like it did when he was chasing me through the streets of Venice until he lost me. I was too quick for him. I should send a thank you to my track coach from high school. "There's nothing to talk about," I say, grabbing an old flyer and shoving it into the copier. I don't know what it is and don't care. Just because I'm not a high-powered executive doesn't mean he can just come and interrupt me at work.

"What is there to talk about?" I ask.

Before I can close the lid to the copier, Flynn intercepts it with a resolute hand. We are both silent, a push and a pull as I attempt to close the copier despite him. I finally give in, ignoring the feeling of his blue eyes on my neck. "Please let me explain..."

"Flynn, really –" I say, starting to laugh. "The whole thing was just madness. Okay? I just want to forget all about it."

He releases the lid of the copier. "Really?" His voice is low and throaty.

"Really," I reply and punctuate my statement by forcefully shutting the copier.

"Is that why you're still wearing the necklace?"

My eyes widen and I fumble to grab the small bird pendant around my neck. I don't have a good excuse for that. It's my way of keeping him close. "We were caught up in the pretend of it all, and I mean, you were there to charm back Adelaide. That was the whole point." I errantly jab the number pad on the copier, accidentally programming it to make three-hundred-thirteen copies. *Shit.* "You got what you wanted."

"That wasn't what I wanted."

"Then why go at all, huh?!" I snap, finally looking at him. *Fuck*. I immediately regret it. Flynn looks so damn good. White dress shirt crisp over his chest, his black glasses framing those gorgeous blue eyes, and his sexy lips... oh, those lips.

He came down here from New York in the middle of his day to see me. Doesn't that count for anything?

The copier starts to sputter out pages. The sound is ugly and mechanical. "From the start, you were using me. That was the agreement. I let the ouzo go to my head. I'll get over it."

"I didn't *use* you."

"Flynn, you got my time, I got your money. Let's not pretend it was anything more than that." I don't believe that with my whole heart, but I have to protect myself. He can't know that I've been aching for him every single moment of the day and night. That I've barely been sleeping because I am dying for the moment he'll crawl into my bed. His ego doesn't need to know that. "I hope you and Adelaide are very happy together."

"Stop acting like you know what I'm thinking!" Flynn suddenly shouts, slamming his hand down on the copier.

I stare up at him with terror. His face is contorted with frustration, red as a tomato.

"All you've done is run from me."

"You don't own me, Flynn! No one owns me."

"And you don't listen either!"

I scoff. "Why are you surprised, Flynn? This is who I've always been. It's why we don't like each other, remember?"

"Is that what you're trying to tell me, Stella? That you don't like me?" He leans over me.

The pull of fear inside me is suddenly overshadowed by want. I could cower away from him. Or I could remain steadfast. "It's worse than that."

"Oh, yeah?"

I grit my teeth. "Yeah. I hate you." When it comes out, it splits my soul in two. It is so close to what I want to say to him. And yet so far.

"Good. Because I hate you too."

Somehow when he says it, it feels like a drug. I want to hear him say it again and again and again until I... until we... "Well, thanks for coming by with that important update, Flynn," I sneer.

In a split second, Flynn grabs my waist and kisses me. I'm powerless to resist him. Why would I when my body has been calling out for him? I know this is so wrong, but I literally can't stop. I lock my arms around his neck and draw myself close to him, and our tongues lash into each other's mouths.

Flynn pins me against the copier with his hips and draws away for only a moment to catch his breath. "Tell me to stop."

"No."

He kisses me again, distracting me while he grabs my thighs and hauls me up onto the top of the copier. "Tell me, Stella. Tell me to stop."

"I don't want you to," I murmur as I slide my legs around his waist, pulling his groin against mine. We have now spent more time apart than we did as lovers, but the body doesn't so easily forget something as incredible as what we had. I press my hand against his navel and slide it into the waistband of his pants. "Do it. Now."

Beneath me, the hot copier keens as it produces useless pieces of paper. I can't make sense of that right now. All that exists is Flynn and me.

I release him from the constraint of his pants, and he rips my panties down to my ankles. As soon as we are free, Flynn doesn't waste a second more. He positions the head of his cock at my entrance, slides his hands around my ass cheeks, and then yanks me onto him. I hold back a yowl of pain and pleasure, the sudden stretch and arousal coming together all at once.

"Sh-sh-sh..." he says in my ear.

And he's right. We are tucked away in the office, the door half-cracked. If a volunteer doesn't come looking for me, an uncaged mutt might. While I love dogs, nothing ruins the moment more than when they stare at you doing the nasty.

I cling to Flynn with all my might, letting him set the speed and the strength. I push my lips against his neck and sink my teeth into his flesh with desperation. He moans deliciously.

This is what we are now doomed to. A hatefuck at my office. What's next? A hatefuck at his? Out of the question. I might run into Colin, and that would be absolutely terrible, especially since I've been avoiding him for three weeks now.

Flynn hooks his arm around my neck, cradling my head in the crook of his elbow. "Look at me, Stella."

My head falls back. I press my lips together in an effort not to moan. It's hard when he feels so good inside me, and he's a perfect, fuckable vision. His eyes are penetrative, and his lips have fallen open. "I..."

"I hate you," I blurt. "Why do you feel so good?" I whimper. "I hate that you make me feel so good." I fall back and brace myself on the lid of the copier. It continues groaning beneath me, vibrations hitting my ass. "Fuck me, fuck me," I say through clenched teeth.

Flynn pushes his whole length inside only to retract it fully out of me. He does this several more times, each time making my eyes roll back further into my head until I feel every muscle in my body constrict, ready to release in a tremendous orgasm.

Just before I can, though, Flynn kisses me harshly, capturing my moan in his mouth. Just like our budding romance, this will be kept a secret.

It's for the best, but my heart breaks that no one will ever know that, yes, for even just one week, he was mine.

Flynn comes too, stumbling forward and pressing his hands against the wall behind me. His hips jolt and he curses into my hair. I wrap my arms around him, holding him close to me. Desperate not to cry. We did this so many times in that short week together. We folded our bodies into one, and I dreamt of getting to do that for the rest of my life.

I'm not proud of it, but I just couldn't help it.

Everything felt so right with Flynn. Until it was just so wrong.

"Please, Stella, listen to me."

I shudder back to reality and push Flynn back by his shoulders. "You have to leave."

His face splits with desperation. "Stella –" Flynn reaches for me.

"Go, just go. Just please go. I don't want to talk to you. I don't even want to look at you. I don't know why I let you..." I pull down the skirt of my dress and draw my legs up under me. He felt so amazing.

Yet I feel so much regret.

Flynn stands for what feels like a very long time just looking at me. Waiting for me to change my mind. But when I don't, he simply nods. "Okay," he says in the smallest, most heartbreaking voice. "Okay, I'll... I'll go."

I am too focused on holding back my tears to watch him go. It is not until I hear the front door shut, sealing me back inside from the rest of the world, that I let myself cry.

I've told myself so many times that I have to stop crying. That Flynn is not a man worth crying over.

It doesn't matter. The tears keep coming as if my body knows something that my mind doesn't.

Chapter 19

Flynn

I've quit working from the office for the past two weeks. I'm done being questioned, done having my suits ripped, done nearly giving my dog an aneurysm.

In fact, I didn't even show up for our presentation. Colin objected, but I thought I'd just get in the way. "Let them look at the tech. Then they can call me with the questions." From everything I've heard, Colin and Rickie did amazing. Colin hasn't said it was better without me there, but it was.

I'm just... a laughingstock.

To be fair, I haven't actually done anything. It's just what the media has purported I've done. I haven't given one singular interview, and haven't so much as spoken to anyone outside the company. And yet I'm constantly being "quoted" or spoken for in magazine articles.

All because Adelaide won't shut up.

We spoke on the phone actually just last week. I finally had the balls to tell her I'd be building a case against her for libel if she didn't shut up. She burst into her usual crocodile tears. "Flynn, we are perfect together, don't you see?!"

The longer I've thought about it, the more I think she's come to understand that Theo is only going to get dumber the longer he plays football. And once he retires, it's all downhill from there. I have always been a long-term investment (as crude as that may be). Now she's just mature enough to see it.

Too bad she pulled out her funds two years ago. I wish I had never laid eyes on her.

Today is a day like any other when I'm working from home. Wake up, take Freckles for a walk through Central Park with sunglasses and a hat so no one recognizes me (hopefully), make a pot of coffee, log on, work the rest of the day, and then...

Dissociate about how badly I fucked up with Stella.

I had no intentions of having sex with her when I went to talk to her. But when she shoots her mouth off like that and makes me so angry, it's impossible to resist her.

I promised Colin. I wouldn't force it. She gave me her answer. She wanted me to leave.

So here I am, carrying around this wound like my life depends on it. As if I let it heal, then that part of me, the part of me that loved Stella, never existed.

In the midst of numbing out and clicking around on my computer as if I'm actually doing anything, I hear the front door click open. Freckles hears it and runs out of the office toward the front door. The only person who has an extra key is Colin, and the only person that could walk in without Freckles freaking out would also be Colin. "Yeah?" I call out from my office.

Colin pokes his head in. "Brought bagels."

"Not hungry, but thanks." Heartbreak has made my appetite nearly non-existent.

He drops a paper bag of bagels on my desk and sighs. "Thought you'd say that."

Freckles sniffs the bagels. I grab the bag and put them out of her reach. "No…"

She huffs in annoyance.

Out of the corner of my eye, I see the cuff of his purple suit. *Purple?* "What the hell are you wearing?" I gasp.

Colin bends his knees and straightens his coat with a smile. "You like it?"

"It's purple!"

He rolls his eyes. "Aubergine, Flynn. Don't you know anything?" He dusts off the dark purple lapels and straightens out the perfectly matching dress shirt. "Cash sent it over for me to wear to the show today."

I swallow. "That's today… I'd forgotten." *No, you didn't, liar.* Colin mentioned it last week offhandedly, and I didn't realize he was actually taking a day off to go to New York Fashion Week to watch Stella walk in Cash's show.

"Obviously. You're not dressed for it," Colin says off-handedly and then disappears out my office door.

I laugh. "Right. Well, good thing I'm not going then."

"Yeah, about that…" Colin calls out. "I think you should go."

Did I just hear him correctly? I look at Freckles. She just cocks her head at me as if I'm an idiot. "And why the hell would I do that?" I ask, getting to my feet.

"Well, it's good to be supportive, don't you think?"

I follow him out into the living room, where he's hooked a garment bag onto a curtain rod and is carefully unzipping it. "What the hell is that?"

Colin smiles at me over his shoulder. "Cash sent this one for you." He tugs the garment bag down and reveals a suit exactly like his, except orange.

"I'm not going to walk around like a tangerine, Colin."

"Close. It's burnt sienna."

I laugh dryly. "Alright, well, no burnt sienna. Besides, I'm not going."

"Come on! She had it made custom for you!"

"How the hell did she get my measurements?"

Colin hesitates and then shrugs. "I've had them for a while, always good to have in a pinch."

"Colin!"

"At least try it on."

I cross my arms. "There's no point in me going."

"But Stella –"

"What about Stella?! She isn't interested in hearing my side of the story. I backed off. That's what you wanted, isn't it?"

Colin sucks in on his lower lip. "Look, you're miserable, Flynn."

I start to object, but he isn't having it.

"You've been a hermit for two weeks straight since you saw her. And…" He shuts his eyes. "Yes, it's still weird that she's my sister and you're my best friend. And *yes*, I don't want you or any man to pressure her into something she doesn't want." He takes a moment and then says definitively, "But if I know you and I know her, I think you're both letting your pride get in the way of actually communicating."

I've known about my pride for a while. But Stella's? I'd never stopped to consider that.

"One more chance. And then we can all leave it alone."

I stare at him. The last thing I want to be is the guy who can't leave well enough alone.

But I do love her. And I want to get the chance to tell her. "Okay."

"Yes! Perfect. You come to the fashion show. We can all celebrate after. If she can't stand you, you get the hell out of dodge, and I owe you big time for the rest of our lives. Or…"

"Or…"

Colin smiles and grabs the suit. "Put it on, put it on!"

I groan but take the suit from him. "You already owe me big time for having to wear this suit. We're going to look like The Wiggles."

"Flynn! It's haute couture!"

"Since when do you care about haute couture?" I ask.

Colin looks away, face flushing. "I don't know, I've always liked it."

I smile. "Does this have to do something with Cash Cole?"

"No!" he says all too defensively. "No, I just…" He straightens up. "Just put the damn suit on!"

I disappear into my bedroom and throw the suit on. It fits perfectly and, I have to say, looks much better on than on the hanger. However, I feel out of place in such a nice suit when my hair is unkempt, and my glasses are askew on my nose bridge. I suddenly realize that this is the first event I'll have been to since everything imploded. Sure, the press could catch me walking in and out of work. But I've rejected invitations to so many things in the name of privacy and staying out of the limelight. Now I'm seriously contemplating going to the LITERALLY most photographed event in the world. There's no way I can do this. "Colin, this is ridiculous."

"Can I come in? Can I see?" Colin waltzes in with his hand over his eyes.

"I'm dressed, dummy."

He drops his hand and gasps in delight. "You look amazing, dude."

"I look stupid."

"You just need a little hair product and to polish the lenses of your glasses. You'll look perfect."

I swallow. "People are going to talk."

"Flynn, look at me."

I look at Colin in the mirror, his head tucked next to my shoulder.

"Fuck 'em."

I can't keep from smiling. A small laugh comes out of me. And then a bigger one. "You're right. Fuck 'em!"

"Fuck all of them. Fuck Adelaide, fuck Theo, fuck People Magazine, fuck TMZ. Fuck 'em!"

I comb my hands back through my hair and then polish my glasses on my sleeve. Even just that gives me a little spike in confidence. "We look like a Thanksgiving cornucopia."

Colin tilts his head to the side. "Yeah. You're right. Better than The Wiggles, though."

We stand there a moment longer. "I'm terrified."

My friend nods. "Yeah, me too."

I take a deep breath and clap my hands. "Great. This is going to be a mess, isn't it?"

Colin begins to open his mouth, but I hold up my hand to stop him. "Don't answer that. Let's just get out of here before I change my mind."

Chapter 20

Stella

"Five minutes, everyone!" the stage manager shouts into the bathroom.

I don't say anything in return, curled up in the corner of a stall with my eyes glued to my phone.

I'm late.

Not just a little late, but really late. At least that's what the period tracker on my phone says. A calendar full of days not marked with red dots where they should be.

I don't usually worry if my period is a couple of weeks off. The pill can cause my cycle to fluctuate from time to time. Sometimes I skip whole months at a time, other times I'm spotting for a week straight.

Except, this time, I'm sick.

Like doubling over the toilet and retching my guts out sick. And it's been this way for three days now.

Even that, I might be able to write off as a stomach bug or norovirus, maybe.

Except my breasts are also sore. Like *so* sore.

Please don't be pregnant, I think to myself.

Not much else I can do but hope right now. I'm trapped backstage at Cash's runway show, the one ostensibly for me and the shelter. I tried one last time to get out of it yesterday when I was bent over the porcelain throne for the fifth time that morning.

Her solution to my sickness? "We'll have a bucket for you offstage. Don't worry, plenty of models have done it before you."

Well. That's just great, isn't it? I'm going to have to walk down a runway in front of hundreds of people I don't know, cameras at me from all angles, trying not to throw up. And on top of all that, I might be pregnant.

Oh God, I might be pregnant with Flynn's baby.

As if this situation couldn't get more convoluted.

The door snaps open again, and I hear Cash's voice. "Stella! Where the hell are you?"

I get up and open the stall door, stepping out into the dingy bathroom lighting. "Here."

"For God's sake, we have to get you dressed! I know you're my muse, but I can't stand a drama queen!" Cash gestures to the changing robe I'm still wearing; I sprinted in here in the middle of makeup when I felt my stomach lurch. Luckily, I was able to quell my nausea with some deep breathing, but I'm still lightheaded.

"I really don't think I can do this, Cash."

Cash ignores me, grabbing me by the arm and yanking me out of the bathroom. "Stage fright. It's normal."

For such a tiny woman, she moves at the speed of a hummingbird's wings. I'm tripping behind her as she takes me back to the makeup chair.

"Alright. Just sit, let them get you all sorted."

I look at my reflection in the mirror. I know my makeup is only halfway done, but it makes me look sick, even sicker than I feel. My lips are blocked out with concealer, and my eyes are rimmed in light gray. We look more like extras in a horror movie than models.

As the makeup artist goes back to her work, dusting a translucent powder over my forehead, Cash stands beside me and softly kneads my shoulder. "You can't let it get to your head."

If only I could tell her that I'm not even thinking about the show anymore. My head is already several hours in the future, wandering through a Duane Reade, trying to get the gumption to pick up a pregnancy test.

"You're the star, Stella." Cash giggles. "It's in your name."

"Cash –" Gregory bumbles over with a look of desperation on his face, holding a broken high heel.

Her façade to calm me immediately drops. "Can't you see I'm busy, Gregory?! Dammit!"

Gregory skitters away. Cash takes a deep breath and tries to reinstate her air of tranquility. "Where was I?"

"Cash, this is your big day. Not mine. You go deal with what you have to deal with. I'll...I'll be okay." That feels like the biggest lie I've ever told. I know I *will* be okay, but it sure doesn't feel like that when I may or may not have a clump of cells dividing inside me at a rapid rate to form another living being, which is causing me the worst nausea and lightheadedness of my life.

"Two minutes!" the stage manager yells.

"For heaven's sake, slap some eyeliner on her and let's go!" Cash shouts at the makeup artist before darting away to deal with a fire somewhere else.

The makeup artist takes out a pot of eyeliner and does her best to create dramatic wings on my lids despite my eyes flinching and watering.

The second I'm done in the chair, Gregory is back, hustling me over to get changed into my first look, a dramatic button-down that has tails down to the floor with cigarette pants and the highest, most uncomfortable shoes in my life. The premise of the show is that with each look, things ease up and become more natural (natural according to Cash Cole, that is).

"Lean on me," Gregory says so he can lace up my high heels. The pants are so tight I can't bend over and do it myself, but that seems to be the norm around here. All the models have handlers flurrying around them, straightening, steaming, and tying.

I grab his shoulder, but tilting the littlest bit forward makes my head spin. I start to topple, bracing my other hand on his back.

"Woah, woah, woah," Gregory says, grabbing the top of my thigh to keep me from falling over. "You really don't wear heels much, huh?"

If only it had to do with the heels and not literally everything else. "Is it that obvious?"

Gregory sighs and shakes his head. "You'll be fine, dear. Get in line."

I teeter over to the line of models that's started accumulating at the entrance to the stage. All of them have their game faces on. Meanwhile, I'm chewing like crazy on my lower lip.

"Put your teeth back in your mouth, you just got your makeup done," Cash says, smacking my tush as she moves to the front of the line.

I leap into the air and yelp before tucking my lips back into a tight line over my teeth.

For the women around me, this is just a normal day at work. For me, this is true torture.

The only good thing is that it's benefiting the shelter. I have to keep reminding myself of that as the arches of my feet start to ache as we wait for the music to start.

I close my eyes and am immediately hit by the image of my mind of Flynn. Usually, I open my eyes back up immediately to avoid lingering on the idea of him for too long. But the image of him right now is strangely comforting. Because I might have a piece of him inside me.

I never planned to be a mother this way. Accidentally and maybe on my own. And yet the idea of having a piece of Flynn entangled with me forever...

"Cash, you're on."

My eyes shoot open. A newfound resolve inside me. This catwalk is more symbolic than that. It's like walking into my future.

What's on the other side, I don't yet know.

But I'm ready to find out.

Chapter 21

Flynn

We make it just as the lights are going down. Our seats are, much to my chagrin, primely located in the front row on the side of the catwalk. As we are led to our seats, Colin turns around and holds out a pair of sunglasses to me. "Put these on," he whispers.

"Colin, I think I'm past the point of being recognized."

"No, it's part of the look. Cash said so."

I hold my tongue and indulge him. Clearly, he's trying to make a good impression, and what I'm currently wearing is the last thing on my mind.

I can feel eyes on me from all corners of the audience. There are going to be pictures of Colin and me all over the society pages after the flurry of photogs caught us walking into the venue. *Ignore them, Flynn. They don't matter.*

I'm here for Stella and Stella alone. This is my final chance to show up for her. Show her that I'm here for her completely and utterly.

We sit just as Cash walks onto the runway. Behind Colin's sunglasses, I can see his eyes light up. He's got it bad.

"I know it's a little unconventional for me to come and welcome you to the show rather than waiting until the end. But this is my most important collection to date. This is a collection that encapsulates what it means to be a woman and contains multitudes. One of our models in particular stands out as someone you are not used to seeing on the catwalks of Bryant Park. Stella Banks, a virtual unknown in this world, and my new muse. An effortless beauty and unwilling to bend herself to convention. Today she is a model, but most days you can find her running Pair of Paws, a no-kill shelter in New Jersey. They are full-up with adoptable darlings, and we need your help in finding their forever homes," Cash explains with an elegant, unquestioning air.

I'm glad Stella found her. At the very least, maybe she won't regret the trip if she got a good friend out of it.

"After the show, join us out in the park to meet some of the animals up for adoption," Cash says and then smiles, folding her hands gratefully. "Enjoy."

Music begins to play, sweeping strings infused with an urban beat. The first models begin to walk down the runway, but I don't even feel like I'm seeing them. I'm just waiting for Stella. Colin beside me is doing enough enjoying for the both of us, on the edge of his seat with his mouth open.

The things men will do for a woman that isn't even theirs.

Finally, Stella walks out, her curls swept back in a tight ponytail and her expression impossibly serious as she keeps her eyes on the end of the runway. Her heels are sky-high, and she's doing an amazing job of walking in them. Her blouse floats behind her like a train.

People around me start to applaud, so I do too, meekly. I feel my strength leaving my body as I'm consumed with nervousness. I hope she doesn't see me. I don't want to throw her off her game.

Models start returning in different outfits. Stella struts out again, this time in an olive dress torn asunder to reveal a T-shirt, complemented by a pair of combat boots. Somehow, she doesn't seem as steady as when she was walking in the high heels. Her cheeks are sunken as if she's sucking on them.

Something's wrong. I can just feel it. I glance at Colin to see if he notices, but he's too caught up in the drama of the show to notice.

She does her walk and then disappears into the back again.

The next round begins; every model is wearing a Pair of Paws t-shirt paired with incredibly crafted pants and sandals. Very Stella all around. Some of them are even walking dogs down the runway.

Stella emerges at the very end. Maybe it's the makeup, but she looks incredibly pale. I know her body well enough to know when she's struggling. Her chest is heaving as she takes measured breaths, walking down the catwalk in her signature Birkenstocks, her hair now tumbled over her shoulders, wild and free.

When she gets to the end of the runway, she strikes a quick pose before she starts back down the runway. Her steps are heavier, as if she's about to trip over her own feet.

"Colin, something's wrong," I say."

"What?!" he asks loudly over the music.

My concern is confirmed when Stella comes to a complete stop and grabs her head.

I get out of my seat as quick as a flash and leap onto the runway just as she wavers and her eyes start to roll back into her head. I grab her before she can hit the ground; she's passed out completely.

There's a collective gasp from the crowd; the music stops suddenly.

I lower Stella to the ground carefully, taking her up in my arms. Then I touch her cheek and rub my thumb across her skin. "Stella... Stella, can you hear me?"

Her head lolls to the side as she takes a deep breath, struggling to force her eyes open. "What's..." Our eyes meet. "Flynn?"

I push the sunglasses up onto my head so she can see me clearly. "Hey. It's okay. You're okay."

"Stella, oh my god, are you okay?" Colin exclaims, falling to his knees.

Her hand tightens on my arm. My heart flutters. "What happened?"

"You don't remember?"

"I..." she shuts her eyes tight. "It's so bright in here."

I look up at Colin. "We need to get her to the hospital."

Colin swallows and nods, pulling out his phone.

Colin and I look like clowns pacing back and forth in the waiting room in our matching suits. He's told me a couple of times that I can go, but there's no way that I'm leaving him here alone. Even if Stella doesn't want to see me, I'll be by my best friend's side as long as he needs me.

He's currently on the phone with Cash. "Everything's fine. Please, you don't have to come out here and check up on her right now."

By the time an ambulance arrived, Stella was alert. She was complaining of nausea and dizziness, but otherwise, she seemed fine. Colin rode in the ambulance with her and I caught a car here.

"Dehydration," her doctor, a middle-aged woman with dark hair and nice smile lines, had told us once she was admitted. "I'm pretty sure it's as easy as that. Happens in her line of work a lot. I do want to run a couple of tests, though, just in case."

We've been waiting for these tests for a while, relegated to the waiting room to let Stella rest and stay out of the way of the doctors.

"Mr. Banks?"

Colin and I both flip around to face the source of the voice, a spritely little nurse with a pixie cut.

"Not me –" I say and then point at Colin. "Him."

"Gotta go," Colin mutters into his phone and then hangs up. "Yeah, me, I'm Mr. Banks."

"Then you must be the daddy!" she says with a giggle and a big grin.

I blink at her. I'm not even sure I understood the string of words that came out of her mouth. "What?"

The nurse's eyes widen. "Wait, you didn't know? I thought you already knew!" She puts her hands against her cheeks in shock. "I'm so sorry, I –"

"I need to sit down," Colin says, his voice cracking.

Then you must be the daddy…is Stella pregnant?

I glance back at my friend, who has his head between his knees. He might be the next one to pass out. Then I look at the nurse. "She's pregnant?"

"Kathy!" Stella's doctor rushes out from around the corner. "You did it again, didn't you?"

"I'm sorry, Frances sent me to get them, I didn't know – I thought they were worried about the baby, I thought it was –"

Their argument fades into the background as I stand there and let the news sink in.

Stella's having a baby. My baby. I don't know whether to laugh or cry. Whatever the reaction is, it's one from a place of joy. Joy I can't quite understand or comprehend right this second. Not as long as I don't know where Stella and I stand.

"I'm sorry, she never should have said anything. There's patient confidentiality, you understand, and –" the doctor says to me hurriedly.

"Can I see her?" I ask. I don't care how I found out. That's not important anymore. All that matters is getting back to Stella.

She sighs. "Room five-thirty-two."

I nod back at Colin. "Could you keep an eye on him?"

"Oh God, he doesn't look good," the doctor mutters, already gravitating toward her next patient.

I wind through the halls to room five-thirty-two. The door is ajar. I stand there for a moment, trying to steady my breath.

My whole life might be about to change. Terrifying and... exciting.

I knock softly.

"Come in," Stella answers in a small voice.

I push the door open and poke my head in. "Hey."

Stella's eyes widen. "Oh, I wasn't expecting you."

"I can go if you –"

"No, don't. Please." She gestures toward the lone chair beside her bed. "Come sit. If you want."

I walk over to the chair and sit down, immediately groaning. "Man, they keep making these things more and more uncomfortable, huh?"

"Wouldn't know. I'm the one in the bed," she says with a half-smile.

I consider her face for a moment and smile. "Color's back in your face."

She touches her cheek. "Oh. Good." Her eyes are looking everywhere but mine. "Listen, I need to tell you something."

"I know, Stella."

"No, not like –" She swallows. "It's like a big something. I just found out myself and –"

"No, Stella. I know." I throw caution to the wind. Fuck it. This woman is carrying my baby. I grab her hand tight and hold it up to my chin. "I already know."

Stella frowns. Her fingers shift in mine as if trying to get more comfortable. "H-how?"

"The nurse spilled the beans. She thought you were here because you were worried about the baby or... I don't know." The word "baby" just slips out, and the second it does, I feel my heart punch up into my throat.

Stella stares into her lap. "I just found out. I promise I wasn't trying to keep anything from you."

"So, it's mine?" I ask softly.

She snorts. "Is that a joke?"

I try to smile. "Only sort of."

Stella looks slightly wounded. That wasn't my intention. "Yes, Flynn."

"Sorry, I didn't want to assume that..." I shut my eyes and shake my head. "I don't know."

"How does it make you feel?"

I lift my gaze and find myself bathed in hazel. "Me? I mean, how do you feel? You're the one who just –"

"I'm not talking about that. I'm fine. I've got an IV, I'm..." She inhales deeply. "How does the news make you feel?"

I could write epic poems about how the news that Stella is pregnant with my baby makes me feel. "I think it matters more how you feel than me." It's her body. She can make her own choices. I don't want my feelings to taint what she wants to do.

"*Flynn*, I'm asking you because I need to know how it makes *you* feel," she says in a whisper, practically begging.

I take a beat, wrapping her hand in both of mine. It's a risk, but what do I have to lose at this point? I've already lost her once before. "Terrified. But the good kind. Because the thought of you having my baby makes me happier than I can even begin to describe."

Stella's eyes widen.

"And if you feel the same, then all I can ask is you let me be a part of it, even just the littlest bit." My eyes well with tears. "I know you hate me, but maybe you could forgive me or –"

Stella pulls on my hands and presses her forehead to mine, effectively silencing me. It's different than a kiss. It's like our souls are connecting just as our bodies already have.

Then, it just spills out along with my tears. "I love you, Stella. Really. I know it doesn't make sense, but –"

"I love you too. I love you so much."

I can't believe my ears. All this time, I thought she hated me, yet the same feelings have been growing in her. Along with a little something else we didn't anticipate.

Stella kisses one of my falling tears away and nuzzles my cheek. "I want to have a baby with you."

I can't resist her a second longer. I kiss her on the lips with all the passion I have in me. Not the kind of intense midnight entanglement, but that of boundless love.

Stella falls into my arms; it feels like she's making a home there. Like she might never leave. And that's just fine with me. She takes one of my hands and puts it up against her navel. "It's still so early. Nothing has really changed, but…"

Right there. Our whole future is growing inside her. I'd do anything to protect it. I smile at her, tears still brewing in my eyes. "Is this real, Stella?"

She smiles back, cradling my cheek in her hand. "I hope so."

"Knock, knock! I have a visitor."

The door creaks open; Colin emerges in a wheelchair pushed by Stella's doctor.

"What happened?" Stella gasps.

"Shock," I say wryly, giving her hand a squeeze.

"We tried to walk here, but he was a little unsteady on his feet, so –" the doctor explains, rolling Colin up beside me.

Colin looks at our entangled hands and then between our faces. "Well," he says with a resigned sigh. "What did I miss?"

Stella and I both laugh.

"Nothing, really," she says with a grin.

"Totally nothing. Just my sister and best friend having a baby together. No big... no big deal," Colin says with a big gulp of air.

I grab my friend by the shoulder. "Hey. I owe you."

Colin smiles at me lopsidedly. He was the biggest champion of the two of us together. He has himself to thank. "I have a few ideas of where to start with that."

"Me too. Stella, can you set Colin up with Cash?"

She grins. "You read my mind."

Colin goes red as a beet. "Now, wait a second –"

"Don't act like you're not already obsessed with her," Stella teases. Then, she subtly squeezes my hand.

There is a lot we have to work through. Not just the two of us, but the three. And then the four. In a matter of an instant, I've gone from a bachelor to a family man.

And there's no other way I'd rather have it.

Because Stella and me? Well, it just makes sense.

Chapter 22

Epilogue

A year and change later...

"Have you got everything?"

"Chef already loaded the picnic basket, towels are on the tender, and –" I slap the side of my bag. "Diaper bag is loaded."

Cash holds out an extra diaper. "Just in case."

I roll my eyes and snatch it from her. She's not wrong. Always better to have too many diapers than not enough. That's a cardinal rule of motherhood. I stick it into the diaper bag. "What are you two going to get up to while we're gone, hm?"

Cash shrugs and glances back at Colin. My brother is enjoying looking out at the deep blue of the Med through binoculars. "I'm sure we'll figure something out."

"God, he's such a nerd," I say.

"I know," she replies with a twinkle in her eye. "My nerd."

I laugh. Colin and Cash were fast friends but didn't start actually dating until last New Year's when Cash invited him to a party... in Melbourne. Colin didn't bat an eye and was on the first plane headed for Australia.

He didn't return for a month.

Now, they split their time between New York and Melbourne. Between their hectic schedules, I'm surprised I was able to get them to carve out a week for a Mediterranean cruise.

"Oh, if Herbie and Otis are hungry, you can give them a handful of dry food, but no treats. And Freckles needs her p-i-l-l at one."

Out of the corner of my eye, the collie raises her head from the pile of dogs sleeping in the sunshine. I swear that girl is learning how to spell.

"Got it. Listen, don't you worry, we got it all covered."

I giggle. "Not sure about that. Alright, I'm off."

"Colin, come on, we're saying goodbye. Put the binoculars down!" Cash calls out.

The three of us walk to the aft deck where the tender is bobbing along. One of the crew members is organizing all our various sundries for the trip. However, the most precious cargo is Flynn holding our six-month-old little girl, Phoebe. I am constant mush watching the two of them together. Flynn has taken to fatherhood like a fish to water–a proud, doting girl dad.

"Look who it is, Phoebs!" Flynn cries out and points at me.

Phoebe wiggles on his lap and claps her hands, reaching for me.

"She's always so excited to see you. What about me, hm? What about Auntie Cash?"

I climb into the boat and take the wriggly baby from Flynn. She's already lathered in sunscreen and donning the most adorable hat patterned with tiny watermelons. "Guess you'll have to have your own!" I say, then relish how both Cash and Colin blush, not looking at each other.

"Alright, well, I want a kiss goodbye!" Cash crouches down the boat and kisses Phoebe's chubby cheek. "Don't get any cuter, or I'll just have to steal you."

Phoebe squeals happily.

I settle into my seat on the boat, tucking Phoebe on my lap. "Alright, wave goodbye!" I take Phoebe's chubby hand and wave it. "Bye!"

Colin and Cash wave from the deck as the tender peels off.

Once the boat gets up to speed, I settle into my seat, curly my legs up under Phoebe and examine the white cast of sunscreen on her face. "Good job on the lotion, Dad. Don't think you missed a single spot."

Flynn smiles and shrugs. "What can I say? One of my many special talents?"

I smile back. Things have been... good. Really good. I mean, probably as good as you can get for doing things as ass-backward as we had. Fake relationship to real relationship, accidental pregnancy to little family. Flynn and I have enjoyed each other every step of the way. Sure, there have been hard moments. I think I accepted that from the start. It would have been foolish to assume it would all be rainbows and unicorns. With Flynn, though, I'm confident that we will always come out on the other side stronger.

We've been through too much together to give up on this.

Plus, Phoebe makes things even better. She's just about the best baby you could ask for, hitting all the milestones right on time with such a good temperament.

I know I'm crazy to even let the thought cross my mind so soon, but I think I want another one asap.

"Smile!" Flynn cries out, holding his phone up to snap a photo.

I grin. "Look at the camera, Phoebs!"

She gurgles and holds her arms out toward Flynn.

Flynn carefully steps across the tender to take a seat next to me. He wraps his arm around my shoulder and kisses me.

I let out a long sigh. "What's that for?"

"Can't I kiss my girlfriend?" he asks and then kisses me again. "Mother of my child?"

Phoebe squeals and grabs onto his shirt angrily.

"What, are you jealous? How could you be jealous?" Flynn exclaims, bouncing Phoebe into his lap, peppering her face with kisses.

I lean my head onto his shoulder and close my eyes. It's all been such a whirlwind. Not just a new relationship and motherhood, but things at the shelter have been better than ever thanks to Flynn's donations and the visibility we got at Cash's fashion show. We've been able to expand our capacity and improve conditions for the animals. The work no longer feels fruitless. Especially since I get to bring Phoebe with me most days. Between our three dogs at home and all the animals she encounters on a daily basis, she basically is growing up in a zoo.

However, I have been in desperate need of a vacation. I had no idea how exhausting motherhood would be.

"Duck."

I blink my eyes open.

"Duck, Stella."

Flynn slides down with Phoebe balanced on his belly, and I follow suit. Phoebe laughs like we're playing a game.

"Why are we ducking?" I ask.

"Paparazzi."

I can't help but laugh. "More of them?"

"I don't understand it," he says with wide eyes. "We're just on a family vacation!"

"In the Med on a luxury yacht with your business partner who happens to be dating a very famous fashion designer. Nothing to see here at all, people."

He rolls his eyes.

"It's your fault, if you recall."

Flynn shakes his head. "You're never going to let me live that down, are you?"

"You kissing Adelaide? No."

"For the last time she –"

"Kissed *you*! I know!"

We've gone in circles over the story. After how everything shook out with Adelaide in the months following, her tell-all People articles and publicity stunts, I'm happy to accept his story as the truth since it's clear she's a total narcissist. In fact, the second we announced Phoebe's birth (a month after the fact), she sent boatloads of flowers. Addressed exclusively to Flynn.

I get a kick out of it now, but at the time, if I had gotten my hands on her, it would have been a brutal sight.

Those maternal hormones. They'll getcha.

"Look, let's not fight in front of the baby," Flynn says playfully.

As for us, people still want more of the story. I'm more of a public figure now, although reluctant. I try to stay out of the limelight.

And, not to toot my own horn, but we are a beautiful little family. Of course, people want our picture.

A short boat ride later, and we're pulling into a familiar place: the grotto in Corfu where over a year ago things between the two of us really solidified. It was Flynn's idea to take Phoebe here. I said she wouldn't remember, and he rebutted, "But we will."

It's hard once you've got a little one not to be too focused on their experiences all the time. All I want is for Phoebe's life to be amazing and splendid in every way it can be. I sometimes lose myself in her.

Thank goodness I have Flynn to keep me grounded.

The tender pulls up to the dock centered in the blue water. Flynn gets out first; I carefully hand Phoebe over to him before climbing out myself. Then, once the tender is all unloaded, the boat drives off, leaving us in the grotto. Just the three of us.

October in the Med is much cooler than at the height of summer. But it's a perfect day to bask in the sun and lounge about, just the three of us.

I unfold Phoebe's play mat nervously. "We'll have to keep a close eye on her."

"She can swim."

I laugh. "Barely."

"She'll be fine. Won't you, Phoebe?"

Phoebe pats Flynn's cheek gently. Such a sweet little girl.

"See, she promises she'll be careful."

I take my daughter from him and pop her onto the mat carefully. "Thank goodness you're not too wiggly yet, hm?"

She laughs as I jostle her foot.

"You hungry?" Flynn asks.

"Starving."

Flynn starts to dole out the contents of the picnic basket. "How does it feel?"

I don't look away from Phoebe. Her eyes are just as captivating as her father's. "How does what feel?"

"Being back here. How does it feel?"

I glance at Flynn. "I don't think it's quite sunk in yet."

He smiles, eyes dropping down toward the rim of his glasses. "Do you feel different?"

"Of course. Don't you?"

Flynn shakes his head. "Everything *is* different, but I don't..." He looks at me harder. "I don't feel different."

Before Phoebe was born, I had a libido that could not be tamed. Flynn had to fight to keep up. Since her birth, it's something we have both had to work toward again. That was part of the reason for this trip. Of course, I'm not ready to leave Phoebe behind with anyone, but embraced the opportunity to remember where all of this beautiful mess came from.

It's reignited something in both of us.

"You know I love you, right?"

"Of course," I smile. "I love you, too."

I've never ever gotten enough of hearing him say those three words. I swear, the day after we found out about the baby, we said it back and forth over a hundred times.

"That hasn't changed, Flynn," I say softly. I glance at Phoebe. She's already sun drunk and dozing off. "It gets stronger every day."

"Good. Good." Flynn goes back to shuffling through the picnic basket. I notice his jaw tightening and the muscles in his neck straining.

"Is everything okay?"

"Hm?"

"Flynn?"

His eyes dart to mine and then away just as quickly. "I'm fine! Everything's fine."

I frown. "Flynn. You know I can tell when you're lying."

"Yeah, it's annoying."

I watch him for a long moment. "You going to tell me, or am I going to have to force it out of you."

His eyebrows jump. "How do you plan on doing that?"

"Brute force."

"I don't mind the sound of that."

"*Flynn.*"

He smiles bashfully and then sighs. "Okay. Fine." He reaches into the basket and produces a small velvet box. It takes me a moment to realize what it is. "I was going to wait, but –"

"Did I just –" I feel my heart racing. "Did I just force a proposal out of you?"

Flynn sighs. "It was going to come out at some point. While we're gone, Cash and Colin are setting up a whole romantic setting for when we get back, but knowing we were going to be out here, I just knew I couldn't wait."

My jaw drops.

"I can get on my knee if you want, but…" he glances at Phoebe. She's sound asleep. Any rocking of the dock might wake her.

"You're proposing," I say again as if realizing this for the first time.

"Are you surprised?"

My lower lip quivers and I nod. I didn't expect it at all. Of course, it's been on our minds since before Phoebe was born. We took things as slowly as we could, but preparing to have a baby together really condenses a timeline for romance. Once she came, the idea of marriage just wasn't a priority anymore.

At least not a spoken one.

Flynn crawls to sit in front of me. "Stella. My star."

I smile. Waterworks are imminent.

"We might have strange origins, but you've made my world so bright. Every day, I look forward to the adventures we'll have together. Every day, I realize as if for the first time how lucky I am that you have chosen me. Given me the greatest gift a person can be given." He gazes down at Phoebe, the best thing either of us has ever done. "We're already a family, marriage or not. But I want to do this for us."

Flynn opens the ring box. An emerald flanked by two brilliant diamonds. It's *almost* too much for my taste, but not quite. It's absolutely perfect.

"Will you marry me?"

I'm about to answer when Phoebe lets out a wail out of nowhere. Her whole body jostles. Flynn and I both go into parent mode. I scoop her up in my arms, bouncing her softly. She immediately quiets down. "Were you scared? Were you having a bad dream?"

Phoebe's chunky hands settle around my neck, her head nestled into my shoulder.

Flynn rubs her back softly. "She really knows how to be the center of attention, huh?"

I kiss her forehead and then look at Flynn. "Yes," I say.

Flynn frowns.

"Yes, to your first question."

He shakes his head, his mind clearing. "Oh! Yes. Right."

I laugh as he pulls the ring out, hand shaking as he slips it on my finger. "Don't drop it, or else it belongs to the grotto."

"That's exactly what I'm afraid of."

The ring settles onto the base of my finger. "Fits perfectly."

Flynn takes my hand, kisses it, and then holds it to his chest. "Looks perfect too."

I delicately turn my palm into his cheek. He rests his face right there tenderly.

We spend the rest of the afternoon entangled together, the three of us. At once nothing has changed, and everything has changed. We're the same three we used to be, but now, something bonds us just that much tighter.

Everything is picture-perfect now.

When we get back to the boat that afternoon, Cash and Colin are furious that Flynn couldn't wait. "I knew he wouldn't make it!" Colin chides while Cash pops the champagne.

Of course, the annoyance doesn't last long. We toast champagne and drink as the sun sets over the Med, passing Phoebe around and talking about plans for the future until we can barely keep our eyes open.

I start to fall asleep, tucked into Flynn's arm as we sit around the bunny pad, Phoebe sleeping soundly on my chest.

"Tired?"

"Hm?"

He chuckles and kisses the top of my head. "Let's get you to bed, Stella."

I shake my head and bury myself further into his embrace.

"Or we can stay right here. Forever."

THE END

Reviews are very important for indie authors. Please consider leaving a review of The Billionaire's Invitation if you enjoyed the book. It doesn't have to be long, just a line or two. Thank you so much!

Thank you for reading The Billionaire's Invitation. If you loved this book you will also enjoy Reunited With My Billionaire.

Reunited With My Billionaire is a Second Chance Brother's Best Friend Romance.

He broke my heart into a million pieces when I was 18. Now I'm his live-in nurse and all I can think about is undressing him.

When I showed up on my first day at the new job and realized my patient was Liam, I wanted to hightail it out of his luxury penthouse ASAP. But that wasn't an option.

Liam Kaminsky was my first love. He's also my overly protective brother's best friend. I wanted him to be my first for everything, practically begged him, but my brother made sure that would never happen.

Helping him regain his strength after a ski accident is what I've been hired to do. But I can't focus. His chiseled body and gorgeous face still take my breath away after all these years.

Our chemistry is still undeniable, and I can't hold back much longer.

But he stomped on my heart before and that still stings. He needs to prove to me that this time will be different...

Buy Reunited With My Billionaire **HERE**.

About Alix Vaughn

Alix adores everything about billionaires: yachts, polo ponies, art collections, international travel and the immense power. Her characters usually come to her during a long soak in a hot lavender-scented bath, while sipping expensive tequila.

Printed in Great Britain
by Amazon